NEW DIRECTIONS 37

In memoriam
GIOVANNI MARDERSTEIG
1892–1977

New Directions in Prose and Poetry 37

Edited by J. Laughlin

with Peter Glassgold and Frederick R. Martin

A New Directions Book

ACKNOWLEDGMENTS

Grateful acknowledgment is made to the editors and publishers of books and magazines where some of the selections in this volume first appeared: for Homero Aridjis, *Montemora* (Copyright © 1975 by Montemora); for J. G. Ballard and Martin Bax, *Ambit* (London); for Andy Clausen, *Shoe Be Do Be Ee-op* (Madness Incorporated, Oakland, Cal.); for Jean Cocteau, *Vocabulaire* (© Editions Gallimard 1922), *Poesie 1916–1923* (© Editions Gallimard 1925), *Morceaux Choisis* (© Editions Gallimard 1932), *Grilled Flowers* (Copyright © 1977 by Grilled Flowers), *Webster Review* (Copyright © 1976 by Webster Review); for David Cope, *The Stars of David Cope* (Nada Press, Grand Rapids, Mich.); for Elizabeth Marraffino, *Outpost* (Copyright © 1978 by Outpost Magazine); for Ron Rodriguez, *The Captains That Dogs Aren't* (Copyright © 1977 by Ron Rodriguez); for Carol Rubenstein, *Poems of Indigenous Peoples of Sarawak: Some of the Songs and Chants* (Special Monograph No. 2, Vol. 21, No. 42, Sarawak Museum, Kuching, Malaysia); for Michael Scholnick, *Mag City;* for H. C. ten Berge, *Modern Poetry in Translation* (London); for Stephen Vincent and Michael McClure, *The San Francisco Review of Books* (Copyright © 1977 by The San Francisco Review of Books).

First published clothbound (ISBN: 0–8112–0695–5) and as New Directions Paperbook 463 (ISBN: 0–8112–9696–3) in 1978
Published simultaneously in Canada by McClelland & Stewart, Ltd.

New Directions Books are published for James Laughlin
by New Directions Publishing Corporation,
333 Sixth Avenue, New York 10014

CONTENTS

WOMAN TO HER
MIDGET LOVER. . . .

EDOUARD RODITI

Some women have been observed to be gifted, like the Japanese nation as a whole, with a passion or genius for miniaturization. Whenever they find anything absurdly or abnormally small, whether a kitten, a dwarf shrub, or a diminutive grandfather clock from a set of antique dollhouse furniture, such women can go into veritable hysterics of sheer delight. Often their home thus tends to become, as the years go by, an extraordinary accumulation of midget treasures, a vast and precarious hoard of utterly useless diminutives that are all too easily broken or mislaid, each breakage or loss then proving in turn to be a tragic event, since what their owner had never dared hope to find can now scarcely be expected to be ever replaced.

One such lady was known, in late nineteenth-century Boston, to have gone into an incurable decline, in her home on Commonwealth Avenue, when her huge husband one day carelessly deposited in "my pianoforte" a white-hot cigar ash that cracked it beyond repair: the instrument that the herculean vandal had so wantonly destroyed happened to be an eighteenth-century spinet made of Dresden china and measuring an inch and a half in height, two in width, and four in length. The husband, a repulsive monster in the eyes of his delicate wife, was a handsome retired naval man, well over six foot tall and, we presume, regrettably well proportioned in every other respect. After the demise of his inconsolable wife, he is said to have been so stricken with guilt that his friends advised him to travel for a while in Europe. There he chanced to meet an equally doll-like

1

and delicate French lady of easy virtue in a Paris glove shop where she remarked admiringly, as she fitted him from behind the counter, on the huge size of his hairy hands. She was an exact replica of his deceased wife, but paradoxically afflicted with a passion for everything huge and with a tendency to squander rather than to collect. His subsequent amours with this siren have now been immortalized in a footnote to a paperback critical edition of one of the novels of Henry James, from whose posthumously published correspondence the Chairman of the English Department of one of our Ivy League colleges has been able to deduce that this retired and widowed sea captain was the original Boston expatriate who posed as "the real thing" for a perceptive fictional study of contrasts between American innocence and European corruption.

As for the deceased wife's collection of miniature bric-a-brac, it continued to rouse, in the widowed sea captain, such a tempest of remorse whenever he returned from his travels abroad to his Boston home that he soon stored it away in cardboard boxes in his Commonwealth Avenue attic, where it was rediscovered two generations later, like the original chambered nautilus that Oliver Wendell Holmes had once owned, in a closet which nobody had opened in half a century. The unsuspecting heir who then found himself the owner of this treasure finally donated it, as a tax deduction, to a Midwestern museum, where the whole collection is now displayed, as a series of well-lit midget period interiors, to admiring crowds of frustrated women who have somehow failed to find as adequate an expression for their secret passion for everything that happens to be preposterously small.

Few women are indeed fortunate enough to understand, in the prime of their life, the real nature of such a dominating passion, and then also to discover as adequate an object on which to lavish their feelings. Countess Humiecka, a Polish noblewoman who lived in exile in Paris a few decades before the French Revolution, was in this respect doubly fortunate. In her girlhood, she had already understood that all normally constituted men could only horrify or disgust her, and the privileged circumstances of her noble birth and of her vast fortune allowed her to meet very soon, in self-imposed exile, her ideal mate, Count Boryslawsky, who at the age of twenty-eight had attained the height of thirty-one inches and revealed no signs of any further growth in stature. Exquisitely proportioned in every other respect, the midget Count was of unusual intelligence and strength for his size, and might have been admired as a wit and a dandy in an exclusive society of aristocratic dwarfs. Unfortunately, he inspired only tolerant amusement or humiliating laughter among his titled peers and would have died of shame at the very idea of making a profession of his misfortune by enrolling in a colony of Lilliputian commoners such as the Empress Catherine of Russia had gathered together for her amusement in an ornamental dwarf village constructed in the park of her palace in Oranienburg, near Saint Petersburg.

An orphan since her infancy, Countess Humiecka had fled her native Poland, soon after attaining her majority, not so much for political reasons as in order to avoid marrying a hirsute high-born giant of a landowner to whom her guardians had unwisely betrothed her in early childhood, fondly believing that no girl in her right senses would fail to succumb to the charms of this heroically pro-portioned representative of the most aristocratic traditions of Po-land. Though she had thus chosen the paths of exile for private reasons of her own, the ravishingly beautiful and immensely wealthy young Countess soon became famous in Paris as the most generous hostess of Poland's exiled political élite. In her spacious reception rooms on the "bel étage" of a magnificent "hotel particulier" that overlooked the Seine from the Quai de Bourbon in the Ile Saint-Louis, she entertained a constant flow of Polish patriots, artists, and writers who sought solace here from the humiliations and homesick-ness of their exile. It was indeed in her Paris home that the virtuoso Jan-Svatopluk Bronislawsky first astounded the world, at the age of five, by playing on the spinet, *allegro con brio* and with breath-taking *pizzicati,* one of those rousing mazurkas that immediately proclaimed him a child genius and, a few decades later, earned him the passionate love of a world-famous transvestite French lady novelist.

Count Boryslawsky had fled Poland for similar reasons. At an age when his fond parents still had good reason to believe that their somewhat small and delicate only son might yet grow to be a man of normal stature, he had become betrothed to a local heiress. Now that he had matured to be a mere dwarf, his betrothed, a buxom young lady, responded only with peals of hysterical laughter to his mere appearance, and displayed an obvious preference for tall and muscular young subalterns of the Guards Regiments of the Russian Imperial Household. Fully expecting her to announce sooner or later that she had jilted him in favor of some herculean rival, Count Boryslawsky knew that the moral code of the Polish aristocracy would then require him to defend his honor by engaging the mate of her choice in a duel. But the very thought of the uproarious laughter that such a duel, between a midget and a subaltern of a Guards Regiment, would inevitably provoke in all aristocratic Polish and Russian circles depressed the poor Count so constantly that he fled to Paris, where he now lived in modest retirement, scarcely ever associating with any of his numerous exiled countrymen.

Rumors of Countess Humiecka's brilliant musical gatherings reached him, however, in his despondent solitude, and he sometimes felt a nostalgic desire to attend one of them, if only to hear the infant prodigy Jan-Svatopluk Bronislawsky play one of his rousing mazurkas, which might bring back to the Count's troubled mind some rustic memories of a happier and more carefree childhood. When one of the Count's cousins, who had recently fled to Paris in order to avoid deportation to Siberia as punishment for his activities as a Polish patriot, suggested one day that the solitary midget accompany him, on the occasion of a traditional Polish religious festival, to the salon of the great hostess, the Count acquiesced, though not without some trepidation.

There are moments when, even in a brilliant gathering, everyone becomes obscurely aware that something mysterious has happened, though nobody has yet been able to observe anything at all unusual. It is as if a spell had been cast on all who are present; clocks seem to stop, like a heart missing a beat, and then to start ticking again, as if nothing had happened. Everyone gathered in the salon of the Countess Humiecka was aware of such a moment when Count Boryslawsky entered it and stood briefly hesitating in the doorway before approaching his hostess in order to be presented to her. She then received him without showing any surprise at his diminutive stature, indeed as if she had known him all her life or had waited all these years to greet him as a kind of promised Messiah, a dream at last come true.

It was indeed love at first sight, miraculously reciprocated. For the first time in her life, the teratophiliac Countess now beheld a man who appeared to answer all her prayers, who failed to horrify or disgust her as all other men. To the dwarf Count, she was likewise a revelation of all the secret hopes that he had ever dared formulate. Without a moment's hesitation, they both understood that they had been fated to meet and, without further ado, to patch up in partnership their oddly broken lives so as to remain together "until death do us part."

Nobody knows how the Count and the Countess came, in the crowd of her guests, to their discreet mutual understanding. Though the Count's first appearance in her salon attracted considerable attention, nobody saw him take his leave later that evening. Soon after the last encore performed by the infant prodigy on the spinet, the Count's young cousin noticed that his midget relative had vanished. For several months, nobody in Paris saw him again, though this in itself inspired little comment, since he was known in general to lead a very withdrawn life. The few who called on him in his lodgings were told that he had returned suddenly to Poland on urgent family business.

As for the Countess, she continued to entertain as regularly and as lavishly the cream of the Paris community of Polish exiles, but an entirely new set of retainers was now running her household and serving her guests. She had indeed dismissed her previous domestics overnight, with generous compensations and recommendations, so that they soon found satisfactory employment elsewhere. In their stead, she now employed a full household of deaf-and-dumb retainers whom she recruited from a charitable institution in which she had suddenly developed an interest; all of Paris now praised her patience and charity in training these unfortunates as domestics who, from the experience gained in her household, would henceforth be assured of a livelihood in other homes where they would easily find employment through her recommendations.

But this great lady's numerous admirers continued, as before, to wonder why she failed ever to choose a fortunte partner from among their discontented throng. Unlike any other great lady of her age, she was never suspected of entertaining any lover. Among Paris wags, she was already known as the Vestal of the Vistula.

One of her admirers, a certain Count Perzinski, was the most persistent of all. An elderly roué, he had a reputation of having once been handsome and an almost irresistible seducer; in his own fond imagination, he was still a veritable Paris whom no Helen could resist. Tall and cadaverously thin, he always dressed in the latest and most foppish styles and, among the ladies of easy virtue of the Palais Royal, was generally known as "that old clothes-horse" and was said besides to have other qualities in common with any flesh-and-blood stallion, though he now relied more often on his purse than on his personal charms for his successes.

Be that all as it may, Count Perzinski had ceased, since the preceding summer, to frequent as assiduously the brothels and stews of the Palais Royal and had now become a regular ornament of the salon of the Countess, whom he pursued relentlessly and unsuccessfully with his advances. The mysterious disappearance of Count Boryslawski coincided somehow with Count Perzinski's decision, in the dead of a particularly cold Paris winter, that the time was ripe for recourse to a more military kind of strategy in his campaign to storm the apparently unpenetrable fortress of the virtue of the beautiful Countess.

On a bitterly cold February night, Count Perzynski therefore approached her home soon after midnight. He knew that she had not been entertaining, that evening, any guests. From the riverbank of the frozen Seine, as he looked up, he saw lights still shining in the windows that he knew to be those of her private apartments. With the skill of an expert but all too mature and, alas, unwelcome Romeo, he then slung a rope over the lavishly wrought railing of her balcony and, once it had been secured by a loop on a trefoil of the ironwork foliage, began to climb up to his goal.

The Countess was in her room, dallying with her newly acquired midget lover. Hearing some suspicious noise outside, she opened the window and asked him to see, from the balcony, what might be happening below. Without being spied by the ascending invader of his privacy, the midget Count was able to recognize his rival and rushed back to report to the Countess the dangers that threatened their secret relationship. In a hurried council of war, they agreed on a plan of action.

"Leave it to me," the dwarf Count concluded peremptorily. "I'll cook his goose so throroughly that he'll never dare mention to a soul what he may have witnessed or experienced here." He then gave the obedient Countess some brief instructions, hurried her out of the room, snuffed out the candles that illuminated it, installed himself comfortably on the sofa where the Countess usually reclined when she chose to rest or meditate alone, and quietly awaited there the arrival of the invader in crepuscular gloom.

The enterprising Count had meanwhile completed his romantic ascent to the balcony. There he found the French window closed, but hesitated only a few seconds before breaking one of its panes in order to insert his hand and open it from the inside by turning the ornate rococo ormolu handle of the "espagnolette" fastening. Like a victorious warrior storming a fortress, he rushed into the dark room, where the dwarf greeted him in sweet but somewhat shrill tones that skillfully imitated the voice of the Countess; uttered with the art of an expert ventriloquist, they appeared however to emanate, like a will-o'-the-wisp, in turn from each corner of the vast and dark room.

"Heavens above! Who comes here to disturb my repose?"

"It's only your most fervent admirer, Count Perzinski, dear Countess," the invader replied.

"Only you? Thank God for that. I feared I was about to be robbed or raped. But why have you chosen this most unpropitious hour, when I happen to be least worthy of any man's admiration? Would that you had come at some other time of the day!"

"But only now could I hope to find you alone. . . ."

"Dear Count," the dwarf replied with a heart-rending sigh, "I have good reasons to be alone at this hour. Every night, at this hour, I'm victim of a sorcerer's spell. . . ."

"A spell . . ." Count Perzinski exclaimed, somewhat bewildered. "But surely there can be no sorcerers now, in our Age of Enlightenment."

"Beware, dear friend, of sharing the foolish beliefs of our age, when the Devil himself sees fit to seduce us by convincing us that he no longer exists! I too, alas, always scoffed when I heard of sorcery. Like you, I thought that all talk of witchcraft was a heritage of a less enlightened past, and I dismissed it all contemptuously as superstitious old wives' tales recounted to scare unruly children into obedience. But I was then punished for my incredulity and must rue it for the rest of my days." The dwarf heaved a heavy sigh, almost a sob, that now clearly came from the sofa, toward which his mournful tones had slowly been guiding his gigantic rival.

In a quixotic mood, Count Perzinski felt that he should offer his services to defend his lady against her enemies, be they of this world or of the next: "But surely, dear Countess, a man of courage and determination can render you some assistance in your distress. My sword is at your command. . . ."

The voice of the Countess uttered another mournful sigh: "Would that I could make use of your courage and your sword! But all the courage of the flower of Poland's nobility would be of no avail. Like you, I once scoffed, as I've said, whenever I heard of sorcery. Then, one day, the great sorcerer Twardowski, whom I had offended with my disbelief, decided to punish me and he cast his spell on me. Ever since, I find myself metamorphosed, every night as the clock strikes twelve, into a big black cat. Until dawn, I remain imprisoned in a cat's form, but still endowed with a human voice and a human mind."

"A big black cat? Nonsense. . . ." Count Perzinski burst out laughing.

"Come closer," the dwarf urged him, "come and sit beside me on this sofa and you will soon be convinced of the truth of my sad tale. Take me in your arms," the wily dwarf cooed seductively.

The rash suitor rushed toward the sofa, where his avid hands, in the dark, fumbled until they found, instead of the enticing feminine form that he had expected, only a warm and much smaller furry mass, in fact the dwarf, covered from top to toe in the heavy fox-fur coat and cap that he generally wore on his rare outings when he had to brave the bitter cold of the Paris streets. The dwarf was indeed no bigger and no heavier than a large cat; his fur coat and cap even gave off a slightly pungent feline odor.

"Oh," the horrified intruder exclaimed. "Can it be true?"

"All too true," the dwarf artfully answered with a sigh. "Until dawn I must remain bereft of everything human except my mind and my voice. . . ." As if shaken with sobs and seeking consolation in Count Perzinski's arms, he began to claw with his nails like a cat at the embroidery of his rival's brocade waistcoat; simulating hysterical sorrow, the dwarf even managed to scratch Count Perzinski's hand.

The mystified would-be seducer gasped. Hurriedly dropping his clawing burden on the sofa to suck the blood from his wounded hand, he rose and rushed to the window, ready to make his escape as he had come. But the dwarf flew at him with a leap that would have done credit to the most agile and ferocious of tomcats: "You have invaded my privacy and gained knowledge of my shameful secret! I cannot let you leave this house to spread news of it abroad!"

Count Perzinski, in his attempts to ward off the furry dwarf's furious attacks, tripped over the curved rococo leg of a small table and crashed to the floor in a flowerbed of broken Dresden porcelain. The dwarf was upon him immediately, mewing diabolically, like a true graymalkin at a witch's Sabbath. Rolling on the floor among the sharp fragments of broken porcelain shepherd and shepherdess figurines, Count Perzinski began to scream in sheer terror. Suddenly, the door was opened and the real Countess entered the dark room, followed by a retinue of deaf-and-dumb servants bearing silver chandeliers of lighted candles. But they were all disguised as ghosts, swathed in white sheets in which they had hastily slit holes, like those of masks, through which they could see. Imitating the grave tones of a judge delivering sentence, the dwarf, from beneath the sofa, now used his ventriloquist's skill to project his voice so that it appeared to come from the leader of these ghostly draped figures: "Infamous seducer! Laugh, if you still dare, at the infernal powers of Beelzebub and Baphomet! Admit that you now believe in sorcery, before the great Twardowski and his familiar spirits punish you by casting a spell on you too!"

In sheer panic, Count Perzinski rushed to the balcony and clambered down to the street, pursued as he fled by a chorus of mewings and satanic laughter. The very next day, he packed all his belongings and withdrew to Rome, where he spent the rest of his days as a recluse, a victim of nightmares and insomnia, never daring to return to Paris or to unburden himself, even to a confessor, of his haunting memories of that one fateful night.

As for the Countess and her dwarf lover, they soon married and, having no further fear of being molested, returned from their Paris exile to Poland, where they lived happily for many years on their estates. At first, such a strange couple inspired of course much gossip in the aristocratic circles that they could not avoid frequenting; but people soon had more novel topics to discuss and even became quite accustomed to the sight of the beautiful countess and her absurdly small husband.

In memory of the musical performance that had first attracted him to her Paris Salon and also of the holocaust of rare Dresden porcelain that accompanied his victory over his gigantic rival, the Countess ordered from Dresden an exquisite porcelain spinet, which she gave the midget Count on the first anniversary of their marriage. It was this self-same spinet, the only one of its kind, that was destined to be irreparably cracked in Boston, one hundred years later to a day, by the white-hot cigar ash of another man of regrettably heroic proportions.

THE IDEA OF VIENNA

WALTER ABISH

BEETHOVEN'S NEPHEW

To please you, I attach
another record of our intimacy.
By noon, next Monday, nothing
will remain in the margin
but the concert notes I have
substituted for your own.
It is unlikely that we'll meet again.

We are, let's face it, far too
responsive to the deliberate enticements
of your mechanical age imagination.
Agreeably we make room for
each fresh mishap, and
encourage more than one
version of everything you decline
to dangle, like an unwelcome
translation from the German,
over the balcony of the former
K. & K. riding academy you
now inhabit. If only

the *idea of Vienna,* that misleading
burst of brilliant scenic relief,
could set a fresh standard for
the glossy postcards mailed to you
with such abandon from the Belvedere.

It might provide a hope for a novel
escape to the American visitor
from New Jersey now attending
the dress rehearsal. I might add,

if one were to reduce your biography
by half, the disquieting thoroughness
of your designs would be forced
to yield all thoughts of spring . . .
I don't know why this need be so,
unless, in taking a last look around,
I may have overlooked
that in the incision of your gloom
lies the reticence of the butchers
who carve into meat
the intricate designs of our utopian needs.

Painstakingly I count the last days
of your life. 721, 722, 723 · · ·
To judge from your expression
I have come nowhere near
exhausting the possibilities
of your unpredictable end.
What are you counting, you asked
out of politeness.
We spoke of nothing but darkness.

By now the extravagant claims
made by the visiting music lovers
are being daily refuted by the
Austrian mountaineers who spend
their long afternoons defecating
on the pinnacles of New Jersey,
and other such mountain ranges.

LOVE LETTER TO LUDWIG II

The fugitive obligations of love,
the emblematic result of your curious
landlocked condition, are wistfully
appraised, then folded again and again,
until the pleats show in the document
of your ornate design.

How fond you have become of meditation
and the grand operatic gesture
which people the empty hallways
with your transient destruction.
You must give upheaval a chance to flourish.
One comes back to the princely obligations.
Is it out of nostalgia?
I regret that we live mountains apart in time
and can only communicate
through the perforated floral tribute,
the scattered thoughts of your set designers
who slave to mutilate the past
splendor of Versailles in plaster of Paris.

As spring carries its edge into the upstairs
parlor, your handsome signature,
suggesting a stable relationship
that has disastrously slipped,
is to be cast into metal for posterity.
At this distance
away from the play area, Ludwig and Wilhelm Richard
have emblazoned on their sweatshirts
their past sibling rivalry:
there's enough to engross all the participants.
For instance

the dangerous manner in which
our castles are toppled,
our collection ransacked,
and the baroque gardens thrown open
to the general public.
Shame we cried, shame, shame.

The mud still clings
to the window sills long after
the set designers have made their escape
from Bayreuth.

It is in this spirit that I set fire to the festival.

GOETHE'S MOTHER

Part 1

Are you planning to inconvenience me
once again in Weimar?
The letter has failed to arrive in time.
It was never mailed. With what alacrity
I face disaster, and vividly employ
the autumn colors of your embrace
with a further postponement in mind,
until the sound of paper tearing
is irretrievably deposited in the rear compartment
of my train of thought.

The pleasant sound of greetings
fails to materialize . . . after all
it is not my business to execute
the daily ceremonies of farewell
and nothing I now say
can possibly convey to you
my doubts at your action.
Even the landscape rises to the occasion . . .
I look out at the bleak mountains
with misgivings.

Are you still standing on the platform
I have left over an hour ago,
waiting to greet me? I cannot help
but view with distaste a performance
in which a group of words,

recited, I suspect, at random for their "poetry"
are strung together
and out of sheer affectation
worn as an ornament around the throat.
I maintain that the word "buffoonery"
has lost its claws.

It can no longer hope to strangle
the ridiculous old woman with a plume
of ostrich feathers on her head,
who said: Je suis la mère de Goethe.

Part 2

The days of the tumultuous parades
have receded in our memory . . . until
their shrill absence caused a famine in our mind.
Does it at all surprise you to discover
how readily we tolerate a change
of pastime.
Purposely I steer the inconclusive discourse
toward mountaintops. Mind you, it is not
the unattainable, only the hypotenuse
of my brain that I wish to recover.

Perhaps the mountaintops on the upper left-hand corner
of the calendar are the very ones Goethe
saw on his Italienische Reise.
We refrain from jumping to any conclusion
about his absence at his mother's funeral.
Yes, we leave him the benefit of our doubt.
It was just one of those unfortunate things
that are bound to happen, explains our stout
English guest.
The "poetry" of each event is chalked up

next to the daily menu of pressed Weimar duck.
Our listlessness, our apathy, our drunkenness,

our lack of affability and participation
are but a successful screen for our surreptitious
longing
for the staged fanfare, the bunting,
and the gaily bedecked omnibuses.
Is it any wonder I no longer care to embrace
our housekeeper Lotte
as she scrawls the words
"Mortification" and "Rage" on the linoleum.

Her madness remains a source
of inspiration for the obese Englishman.
A poet, he sleeps with her every afternoon.
We are too discreet to mention it
in the evening, but the complacent attitude
of my friends places an unendurable burden
upon me.

Last Friday, Frank showed up minus a leg.
It was quite painless, he assured me.
I hardly looked up, he said,
from the book I was reading.
In all solemnity, I must question
the missing furniture,
the stationmaster's unfriendly greeting,
and the bottomless hunger in our hearts.

AN INTERVIEW WITH
MICHAEL McCLURE

STEPHEN VINCENT

SV: You've mentioned the sense of spirit that pervaded the an-
archists and the early printers of the 50s and maybe from there go
on to what you sense is occurring today. There was the influence of
the anarchists in the late 40s and 50s. There was also an atmosphere
here which was anti-Eastern in the sense that people weren't going
to be determined by corporate lives in New York. There was a sense
that you could shape your own life out of what you could provide
from your own self and from the people that you worked with.

MM: The feeling here was not anti-Eastern, but there was, and
is, a major difference between the West Coast and the East Coast,
and it was even more pronounced in the 50s. Northern California
was in the midst of visible nature, and the Eastern urban centers
were centered in what was then, as it is today, an industrial sprawl.
There was the industrial basket, so to speak, of cinders and concrete
and machine construction and old politics and overpopulation on
the East Coast, but in San Francisco we find that the city is the
center of spokes that lead to many aspects of California nature.
From San Francisco you can go to Mt. Tamalpais, to Mt. Diablo,
you can go to the Sierras, you can go to the desert, you can go to
the Valley, you can go to the foothills, and you can go to the south-
ern or northern California coast. San Francisco has access to all of
those aspects of nature. Also, San Francisco is in proximity to Seattle
and to Los Angeles and San Diego, all of which are ports to the
Orient. When you came to the West Coast in the 50s you were, if
anything, more sharply aware of the proximity of the Orient than
you are today when the Orient has made some impression on the

East Coast also. When you came to San Francisco in those days you were aware of the Pacific Ocean, and the Pacific Rim, and the way it was edged with chaparral and redwoods. With nature visible there is an entirely different concept of self. The concept of self in a city of nine million is very different from one's self-image in a city of five hundred thousand with immediate access to deserts and the sight of deer walking through oceanside meadows.

SV: Along with that there was also the requirement of creating a vocabulary, a new language that would work here. There were the precedents of people like Rexroth, all the way back to Joaquin Miller, but at the same time you had to seek out a definition that would work in this new space. Was that part of the angst that was present? There was a kind of romantic pleasure in coming to the West and having all of these—Mt. Tam, the Sierras—at the same time. Didn't it present some kind of terror combined with the excitement?

MM: A terror? No. But there fierce, wild, alien places. And we were all aware of them.

SV: For example, I've heard descriptions by Easterners of the first trip they take down the coast of Big Sur.

MM: I wasn't an Easterner. I was born in Kansas. You were born in Port Richmond, Steve, so you're a Westerner. Gary Snyder was born in San Francisco, Robert Duncan was born in Oakland. I didn't feel terror of nature. I was with Jack Kerouac when he spent some time in Lawrence Ferlinghetti's cabin in Big Sur. Jack was in a state of terror sometimes, but it was not from nature as much as from a dark night of the soul abetted by the horrors of drinking.

SV: Maybe terror's the wrong word.

MM: Not entirely.

SV: In truth, you worked closely with a number of biologists, people in the life sciences.

MM: Yes, many of my friends of this period were people in the sciences. Sterling Bunnel, a visionary biologist, has had a lasting influence on my thinking.

SV: It's not very often that someone's able to get attention as both a poet and a playwright. I'm curious—do you see them, not as simultaneous, but as connected events, or did you move from poetry into plays because you felt poems weren't working on a certain level that you thought a play could. How do you see the connection?

MM: I find that writing poetry and writing theatre are complementary. They don't compete with each other. They use separate parts of the ego. The part of the ego that creates poetry is a sensitive organ that almost wishes to protect itself through the creation of art. And the part of the self that writes theatre is a probe that likes to deal with projections of reality. So I find that the two are complementary, and as I write theatre, I write more poetry, and as I write more poetry, I write theatre. They mutually reinforce each other without feeding on the same interface of creativity. I consider myself a poet. Lately I've been called a poet/playwright so often I've begun to accept the tag, but I think of myself as a poet.

SV: You suggest there are differences in what can happen to language on the page, language spoken, and language as theatre.

MM: Yes, I don't think theatre is meant to be read. We read plays because a play that we want to see is not being performed. But one of the things poets often ask me, when they write their first play, is where they can get it published. I say, don't get it published, get it performed. It doesn't matter on the page. It doesn't really live on the page. The page is like the DNA. You pass it around to theatres and you hope it turns into RNA and you can have an organism—a live play.

SV: How do you want the poem to work on the page? I hesitate to use the word "work" because of several connotations.

MM: How do you want it to play on the page?

SV: Dance on the page. These are all physical images and it seems that somehow just the fact of the page, the print on the page, betrays the physical intentions of what is often being indicated in the poems. I think perhaps in the theatre there is a greater field of expression possible. One of the excitements, or one of the advantages of working with local publishing people, especially people who have access to various types and have a good design imagination, is that you can get a poem out on the page in a way that amplifies the spirit with which it was originally spoken. You can give the words their play.

MM: Let me clarify a point. Theatre is not a matter of words. When I say that a play of mine is a poem I don't mean that the words make up a poem. If you look at the words in a play of mine done here last year, *The Grabbing of the Fairy* (I consider it one of my finest poems), the words on the page are silly. The play is three naked girls with long, furry tails discussing the nature of reality in ritualized combats with one another while an apparition in the form of a giant caterpillar bursts through the wall. The reason that the words of the play are not a poem is that in theatre it is the-organism-in-action of the play that is a poem. The theatre poem is the bodies in action, the movement of the characters, their rites, their speeches, their songs, their conflicts are the poem. Not the words. The words are a part of it. My play *The Beard* is a poem because Billy the Kid and Jean Harlow are in conflict about the nature of what is Divine. The words they use join with the shape of the actions.

SV: Then we see words in relationship to your body in the process of creation as a . . .

MM: I see my poems as extensions of my physical body. That's the doctrine that I learned from the Abstract Expressionist painters. Jackson Pollock and Clyfford Still are painting spiritual, autobiographical extensions. My poems, although they're far from Abstract Expressionist poems (are very concrete poems generally) are extensions of my body. In theatre you have an entirely different situation. The poem in the theatre is the play that's presenting itself in its enaction—as it happens on stage. The director is the RNA and the actors are the proteins; the designers are the golgi bodies; the tech people are the mitochondria—however you want to see it in a biological metaphor. A play is a real physical body that exists for an hour or two in real time and space. It comes together each night that it's performed, and it exists and dances and sings in the symbiotic body that it is. It's a real and true spiritual occasion. Afterwards it's collapsed, folded up, and the scenes are put away, and it never quite exists the same again, and yet somebody, sooner or later, takes out the pattern that the poet/playwright made, and they revive the play.

SV: Let me go back a second to the poem on the page. When you place the poem on the page, how do you want it to be heard? What do you want to occur? How do you want me to experience it?

MM: Twenty-five years ago, there was little chance of the reader of the poem ever hearing the poet. Nowadays there's a good chance when you read a poem on the page that you have either heard the poet reading or have seen a videotape, or heard a recording of the poet.

SV: I've been reading your poems for the last few days, and because I've heard you read a lot, I do hear your voice as I read. It's a larger event than if I'd only experienced it on the page.

MM: I like it most when I've read a poet's poems and then hear the poet. I love the experience of reading the poems and then having the sound corrected, tuned into the poet's voice.

SV: How much was Dylan Thomas an influence?

MM: Thomas was a potent influence on people of my generation. Many people were introduced to poetry by Thomas's recordings. Thomas's readings are more beautiful than the poems themselves. The style of Thomas as a singer enhances the limitations of the poems themselves.

SV: I get the feeling that Thomas's readings in this country in the 50s were a really large influence on the whole.

MM: They were. Bob Zimmerman changed his name to Bob Dylan—a very clear statement.

SV: I want to go back to the question of the poem on the page— of how you write the poem, of how it initially occurs, and of how you choose the structures that you use. I've noticed that in your poems there's a symmetry involved.

MM: Yes, the poems are on a center axis so they look like a little whirlwind or a gyre. They have the bilateral symmetry of an organism. I write the poems that way. I just wrote a play in verse, and the entire play is accurately centered in the manuscript. It happens that way in both handwriting and typewriter composition. The style answers a need. There are numerous reasons why I break a line, and the centered poem has answered the root requirements. I've come to intuitively think in terms of the centered line. We are centered organisms, in the sense that we're bilaterally symmetrical, so poems come out that way with ease and naturalness. Since writing my long poem *Antechamber*, which will be published this spring by New Directions,* my poems have begun a dance on the page. They dance away from the center axis. And as I write poems now that are dancing around the center axis, I find they are a biological extension of my new body condition. As I write them they appear as a dance in the manuscript. That does not mean that I do not learn from other people. In the case of *Antechamber*, which whirls around the center axis but is not fixed on the center axis, I was helped by Maria Epes. When she published it in limited edition as a Poythress Press book, she set up some changes allowing more than the several axes that I was using. I was immediately taken with the beautiful placement on the page. It increased the dance of the words, and I accepted the grace of her sensibility. It opened me to new poems that are whirling or dancing about the center axis. Originally, in the 50s, my poems were only roughly centered and swayed back and forth on the page. In the Auerhahn publication of *Hymns to St.*

* Spring 1978.—Ed.

Geryon and Other Poems you'll find that they're not strictly centered on the page but they're swirling, as they go down the page, from side to side. It's as if they're drunk, mad, impetuous creatures. I realized after we began to be anthologized and appear in commercial books, that I could never get the patience that I'd had from Auerhahn Press. I decided to suspend poems on the center axis, or else the future would do bizarre things to the poems in trying to approximate their swirl and the poems would be bastardized. I went to a firm center axis, and within a few years I was thinking on a centered axis. Finally, whole verse dramas come out precisely on the center. I find that the poem is so much where I am at because the best of my thinking is done through poetry. I don't write a poem and then center it. It comes out centered, and if it doesn't come out centered I'll publish it uncentered. That doesn't mean that I don't make changes, corrections, or variations.

SV: So when you're writing you're actively responding to this sense of the axes?

MM: Yes, it's a physical response, a very pleasurable response. It enables me to feel even more strongly the awareness that I think—as Einstein said that we all do—with our bodies, not merely with our brains.

In *Antechamber* I was using numerous axes. She opened some additional axes that I hadn't seen before. She gave her intuitive understanding of the steps of the dance on the page. As the inventor of the dance, I was restricted by my past concepts, I had held myself back. Wesley Tanner has been a great help to me both as a friend and as a gifted designer. Many times I've had a typographical problem and gone to Tanner for advice. *How will I deal with this use of capitals? With this line of noncapitals?* or, *How far can a line go before I must break it in its publication?* Often I've gone to printers and many times seen printers do very beautiful things for me. Graham McIntosh took my poem *The Surge* and separated out its stanzaic patterns and published it as a small book for Frontier Press. It's not a way that I'll continue to publish *The Surge*, but it's a way that I've enjoyed.

SV: You once suggested that I look at that Dover Press art book publication of Ernst Haeckel's *Art Forms in Nature*. It's mainly sea creatures.

MM: Yes. Haeckel's primary study was of free-swimming jellyfish which are known as medusas. His general field was evolution and phylogeny. He was a popularizer of Evolution.

SV: The symmetry of the creatures he portrays in his drawings is wonderful.

MM: Haeckel is a visionary like William Blake. They are at opposite ends of the nineteenth century. Haeckel is at the *fin de siecle,* and at the other end there is Blake dying in 1827. Blake did drawings of real angels of the imagination, and Haeckel did angelic drawings of real living beings. Haeckel's were jellyfish resembling protoplasm temples, and Blake's were spirits of his own perceptions.

SV: That's what you do in your work—connect with both the angels of the imagination and a radiant sense of the actual.

MM: That's a beautiful way to say it.

SV: I'm struck going through your plays with the way they seem to come from a very futuristic place.

MM: My plays are in some cases more understandably complete organisms than my poems. This does not mean any dissatisfaction with the poems, but I want the poems to be living creatures like medusas broken away from a colony and swimming away in the waves—as if I was the colony and the poem was one of my heads, moving to find a new life of its own—to give pleasure, or awareness, or perception to another consciousness out there in that sea of the universe. Sometimes when I see a little play, like *The Grabbing of the Fairy,* on the stage, I say, *there! now everyone can see that's an organism!* It's on a shelf which we call a stage, and it's moving around in the light, and it's dancing and singing. Surely no one can deny that is an organism—except, of course, the drama critics who will not only deny that it's an organism but give me a moral lecture.

SV: Why do they deny that it's an actual organism?

MM: They begin by denying it is a play because it's not like Clifford Odets or Eugene O'Neill, which is the last thing I want it to be like. The dramas that I value are poetry. I don't enjoy "traditional" recent theatre. I have a strong feeling for the theatre of Aristophanes, the Greek comic poet, the theatre of John Ford, John Webster, Shakespeare, Federico García Lorca, Artaud, Genet, or Samuel Beckett, and others such as the Japanese Zeami, Yeats, or Sophocles. There are wide snowy continents between Arthur Miller and Aristophanes.

SV: Let's go back again to Blake and Haeckel. It seems to me that your poetry, not always but sometimes, is in contact with the immediate universe. If you're in a situation you respond to it.

MM: I'm an atheist but I have the highest respect for the religious experience. I've come to realize that the entire universe itself, and all the universes and all the dimensions of the universe that any of us can conceive of or that may exist or may not exist—all of it, as Whitehead saw it, is the Messiah, and that we only have our redemption, our freedom, our continuation, and our death in contacting, in touching, rubbing against, brushing against, being part of, and expressing ourselves in, and of, the universe. It is all what is called the *Tathagata*. All the *dharma dhatu* is the Messiah. Our contact with it both creates it and expresses it. Or, as Whitehead suggests: we're all moments of novelty in the universe. At any given point we are the universe's awareness of itself. The universe is the absolute nothingness of real Buddha stuff—that's what I believe.

SV: So your poems are moments of novelty.

MM: They're proportionless bagatelles of experience. In looking at a buttercup or by holding a rock in my hand, or in going for a run on the beach, or in walking on Mt. Tam and feeling the sun on my back, and in looking at the deer who no longer even bother to run—I feel myself. That's what I write about.

SV: Well, when people go to your plays, like *The Grabbing of the Fairy,* and say, *I've never seen anything like this, give me back my Eugene O'Neill or my Arthur Miller,* what are the consequences of the organism that you've filled up on the stage? You speak of it as though it's real. It is real and at the same time there are always people out here who will ignore, or give you lectures, saying that it isn't real. . . .

MM: There are some people who love it.

SV: Do you see yourself as a visionary in the sense that the images that you're generating will be, twenty years from now, as current as some images that were created in the 20s by the Dadaists and were considered totally bizarre?

MM: That's possible. The most beautiful compliment I've had was on some of my *Gargoyle Cartoon* plays. Someone came to me and said that they felt when they were seeing the *Cartoons* that they were enjoying classics of the future. I was enormously touched. I've had good luck with directors. They must be seers. My work with John Lion has been one of the best experiences. Having my *General Gorgeous* done at ACT with Ed Hastings as director is a stroke of good luck. If you wrote a play and saw it produced you'd understand why the theatre was sacred to Dionysus. It is like the joy of drunkenness to not only create your hallucinations but to turn them into living organisms, dancing and prancing and laughing and singing upon the stage. You sit in the audience with other people watching with wonder and delight, shock and horror going through your nervous system. It's a rare and beautiful gift, and it is like being the universe. You and I, as organisms, are expressions of the substrate that we walk upon, and the substrate is enormously more complex than we can conceive of because we only think in terms of matter, and not-matter, and time, and space, and light, and dark. It's much much more complicated than that. That's only the surface of it—as we come out into being as organisms expressing that substrate. On having a play, that's a poem, come out of yourself, you kid yourself, you say you're expressing yourself and there it is, that you're watching it, and that you're privileged to sit in the audience and watch your hallucinations. But *in fact* it comes from much farther back, deeper than that. The universe reached through itself to present you as a "movement of novelty." And then the universe, in all of its reason and unreason, has reached through you—and through those other people—and plunked down a living organism on stage. You're there laughing at it, and singing with it, and enchanted with it, thinking that it's yours—but, on the other hand you know that the universe's hand reached through you, far, far, far, farther back than you ever dreamed, and the manifestation of the play in terms of your hallucinations and authorship was merely a convenience that the universe bothered with.

SV: So you don't believe in the Messiah?

MM: I believe it's the universe, which, by the way, is Haeckel's view. He called it Monism. It is a lot like Hua-Yen Buddhism.

SV: Well, tell us what the hand is going to bring us after the turn of the year.

MM: The hand is going to lay out on the stage of the Julian Theatre a play called *Goethe: Ein Fragment.* It is about an imaginary life of Goethe, in which Goethe is approached by Mephistopheles with the proposition that he write a play on a Faust theme.

SV: Is there a printer in the play?

MM: There are two guillotine makers in the play, and they operate a piece of their machinery.

EIGHT POEMS

VITTORIO SERENI

Translated from the Italian by Frank Judge

ALGERIA

At first you were in pain
I could watch in my hands
ever dryer from your dust
so I wouldn't know more of other suffering.
As you search me returned fever
that I missed and in the eternal mirror
you now flash me,
so indescribable signs from ships
break the day in the black harbor
. . . .

AVENUE LODI

Now—said G. dissolving into a yawn—
now leave these things if you can
in the cold galleries of fake paintings and worthless smearings,
the long hairs and the long robes.
Leave it if you can once and for all
the gloomy crowd that sniffs an ornamental truffle
the mob of marxexistentialist
existentialmarxist berets.

And once more deluding myself
that it was really for the last time
on the bridge that crosses over the fog of the city
where the year melts into embers and ashes
I followed him.

IN ME YOUR MEMORY

In me your memory is just
a swish of bicycles that pass
quietly there where the height
of the afternoon descends
to the most flaming evening
between gates and houses
and sighing slopes
of windows reopened on the summer.
There remains, of me, just
the distant lament of trains,
of souls that leave.

And there lightly you leave on the wind,
you lose yourself in the evening.

THE INTERIM

Here's the worm in the woodwork
a thirst renewing itself obscenely
and where love was the leprosy
of the torn walls of the ruined buildings:
a broken city horizon.
Why don't the welders come
why are the repairmen late?
But it's not poor public works,
time has died to shovel under as fast as possible.
And you, how many years to understand it:
too many to be certain.

AN ITALIAN IN GREECE

Early evening in Athens, a long goodbye
from the convoys filling across your borders
loaded with anguish in the long semidarkness.
Like a sorrow
I have left summer at the bend
and tomorrow is a sea and a desert
without seasons.
O Europe, Europe, watching me
step down defenseless and absorbed in my
slender myth among the swarm of brutes,
I am one of your sons in flight who knows
no enemy if not his own sorrow
or some revived tenderness
of lakes and leaves behind lost
footsteps,
I am dressed in dust and sun
I am going to condemn myself to years buried in sand.

Piraeus, August 1942

POEMS

One still writes some.
You think of them lying
to the anxious eyes that wish you well
on the last night of the year.
You write them only in the negative
in a darkness of years
like repaying an annoying debt
owed for years.
No, the job is no longer happy.
Some laugh: you wrote for Art.
Not even I wanted this, wanting something quite different.
You write poems to shake off a burden
and move on to the next one. But there's always
some burden too great, there's never
one line that will be enough
if you yourself forget it tomorrow.

SIX IN THE MORNING

Death, we know, unseals everything.
And in fact, I was returning,
the door was ajar
the shutters barely drawn.
And in fact I'd only been dead a while,
undone in a few hours.
But I saw what surely
the dead don't see:
the house visited by my recent death,
just slightly bewildered
still warm with me who was no longer
the locking bar broken
the bolt useless
and the air great and swarming around
me tine in death,
one after the other the avenues of Milan
awake anchored in all that wind.

TO YOUTH

There has begun a sinister song
of frogs among the hills
and from a mortal summer
—perhaps your last—
swallows in flight rush
desperately, like you walk
toward a deep, wintry, air.

And of the voices that linger
with me, which
will be able to turn your path and mine
to a march of sleepless sunflowers?

But they know no other good or other evil
than a blue or gray lake
your eyes from the shadow of an avenue.

THE INTENSIVE CARE UNIT

J. G. BALLARD

Within a few minutes the next attack will begin. Now that I am surrounded for the first time by all the members of my family it seems only fitting that a complete record should be made of this unique event. As I lie here—barely able to breathe, my mouth filled with blood and every tremor of my hands reflected in the attentive eye of the camera six feet away—I realize that there are many who will think my choice of subject a curious one. In all senses, this film will be the ultimate home movie, and I only hope that whoever watches it will gain some idea of the immense affection I feel for my wife, and for my son and daughter, and of the affection that they, in their unique way, feel for me.

It is now half an hour since the explosion, and everything in this once elegant sitting room is silent. I am lying on the floor by the settee, looking at the camera mounted safely out of reach on the ceiling above my head. In this uneasy stillness, broken only by my wife's faint breathing and the irregular movement of my son across the carpet, I can see that almost everything I have assembled so lovingly during the past years has been destroyed. My Sèvres lies in a thousand fragments in the fireplace, the Hokusai scrolls are punctured in a dozen places. Yet despite the extensive damage this is still recognizably the scene of a family reunion, though of a rather special kind.

My son David crouches at his mother's feet, chin resting on the torn Persian carpet, his slow movement marked by a series of smeared handprints. Now and then, when he raises his head, I can

29

see that he is still alive. His eyes are watching me, calculating the distance between us and the time it will take him to reach me. His sister Karen is little more than an arm's length away, lying beside the fallen standard lamp between the settee and the fireplace, but he ignores her. Despite my fear, I feel a powerful sense of pride that he should have left his mother and set out on this immense journey towards me. For his own sake I would rather he lay still and conserved what little strength and time are left to him, but he presses on with all the determination his seven-year-old body can muster.

My wife Margaret, who is sitting in the armchair facing me, raises her hand in some kind of confused warning, and then lets it fall limply onto the stained damask armrest. Distorted by her smudged lipstick, the brief smile she gives me might seem to the casual spectator of this film to be ironic or even threatening, but I am merely struck once again by her remarkable beauty. Watching her, and relieved that she will probably never rise from her armchair again, I think of our first meeting ten years ago, then as now within the benevolent gaze of the television camera.

The unusual, not to say illicit, notion of actually meeting my wife and children in the flesh had occurred to me some three months earlier, during one of our extended family breakfasts. Since the earliest days of our marriage Sunday mornings had always been especially enjoyable. There were the pleasures of breakfast in bed, of talking over the papers and whatever else had taken place during the week. Switching to our private channel, Margaret and I would make love, celebrating the deep peace of our marriage beds. Later, we would call in the children and watch them playing in their nurseries, and perhaps surprise them with the promise of a visit to the park or circus.

All these activities, of course, like our family life itself, were made possible by television. At that time neither I nor anyone else had ever dreamed that we might actually meet in person. In fact, age-old though rarely invoked ordinances still existed to prevent this—to meet another human being was an indictable offence (especially, for reasons I then failed to understand, a member of one's own family, presumably part of some ancient system of incest taboos). My own upbringing, my education and medical practice, my courtship of Margaret and our happy marriage, all occurred within the generous rectangle of the television screen. Margaret's insemination was of course by AID, and like all children David's and Karen's only contact with their mother was during their brief uterine life.

In every sense, needless to say, this brought about an immense increase in the richness of human experience. As a child I had been brought up in the hospital crèche, and thus spared all the psychological dangers of a physically intimate family life (not to mention the hazards, aesthetic and otherwise, of a shared domestic hygiene). But far from being isolated I was surrounded by companions. On television I was never alone. In my nursery I played hours of happy games with my parents, who watched me from the comfort of their homes, feeding onto my screen a host of video-games, animated cartoons, wild-life films, and family serials which together opened the world to me.

My five years as a medical student passed without my ever needing to see a patient in the flesh. My skills in anatomy and physiology were learned at the computer display terminal. Advanced techniques of diagnosis and surgery eliminated any need for direct contact with an organic illness. The probing camera, with its infrared and X-ray scanners, its computerized diagnostic aids, revealed far more than any unaided human eye.

Perhaps I was especially adept at handling these complex keyboards and retrieval systems—a fingertip sensitivity that was the modern equivalent of the classical surgeon's operative skills—but by the age of thirty I had already established a thriving general practice. Freed from the need to visit my surgery in person, my patients would merely dial themselves onto my television screen. The selection of these incoming calls—how tactfully to fade out a menopausal housewife and cut to a dysenteric child, while remembering to cue in separately the anxious parents—required a considerable degree of skill, particularly as the patients themselves shared these talents. The more neurotic patients usually far exceeded them, presenting themselves with the disjointed cutting, aggressive zooms, and split-screen techniques that went far beyond the worst excesses of experimental cinema.

My first meeting with Margaret took place when she called me during a busy morning surgery. As I glanced into what was still known nostalgically as "the waiting room"—the visual display projecting brief filmic profiles of the day's patients—I would customarily have postponed to the next day any patient calling without an appointment. But I was immediately struck, first by her age—she seemed to be in her late twenties—and then by the remarkable pallor of this young woman. Below close-cropped blonde hair her underlit eyes and slim mouth were set in a face that was almost ashen. I realized that, unlike myself and everyone else, she was wearing no make-up for the cameras. This accounted both for her arctic skin tones and her youthless appearance—on television, thanks to make-up, everyone of whatever age was twenty-two, the cruel divisions of chronology banished for good.

It must have been this absence of make-up that first seeded the idea, to flower with such devastating consequences ten years later, of actually meeting Margaret in person. Intrigued by her unclassifiable appearance, I shelved my other patients and began our interview. She told me that she was a masseuse, and after a polite preamble came to the point. For some months she had been concerned that a small lump in her left breast might be cancerous.

I made some reassuring reply, and told her that I would examine her. At this point, without warning, she leaned forward, unbuttoned her shirt, and exposed her breast.

Startled, I stared at this huge organ, some two feet in diameter, which filled my television screen. An almost Victorian code of visual ethics governed the doctor/patient relationship, as it did all social intercourse. No physician ever saw his patients undressed, and the location of any intimate ailments was always indicated by the patient by means of diagram slides. Even among married couples the partial exposure of their bodies was a comparative rarity, and the sexual organs usually remained veiled behind the most misty filters, or were coyly alluded to by the exchange of cartoon drawings. Of course, a clandestine pornographic channel operated, and prostitutes of both sexes plied their wares, but even the most expensive of these would never appear live, instead substituting a prerecorded filmstrip of themselves at the moment of climax.

These admirable conventions eliminated all the degrees of personal involvement, and this liberating affectlessness allowed those who wished to explore the fullest range of sexual possibility and paved the way for the day when a truly guilt-free sexual perversity and, even, psychopathology might be enjoyed by all.

Staring at the vast breast and nipple, with their uncompromising geometries, I decided that my best way of dealing with this eccentrically frank young woman was to ignore any lapse from convention. After the infrared examination confirmed that the suspected cancer nodule was in fact a benign cyst she buttoned her shirt and said:

"That's a relief. Do call me, Doctor, if you ever need a course of massage. I'll be delighted to repay you."

Though still intrigued by her, I was about to roll the credits at the conclusion of this bizarre consultation when her casual offer lodged in my mind. Curious to see her again, I arranged an appointment for the following week.

Without realizing it, I had already begun my courtship of this unusual young woman. On the evening of my appointment, I half suspected that she was some kind of novice prostitute. However, as I lay discreetly robed on the recreation couch in my sauna, manipulating my body in response to Margaret's instructions, there was not the slightest hint of salaciousness. During the evenings that followed I never once detected a glimmer of sexual awareness, though at times, as we moved through our exercises together, we revealed far more of our bodies to each other than many married couples. Margaret, I realized, was a sport, one of those rare people with no sense of self-consciousness, and little awareness of the prurient emotions she might arouse in others.

Our courtship entered a more formal phase. We began to go out together—that is, we shared the same films on television, visited the same theaters and concert halls, watched the same meals prepared in restaurants, all within the comfort of our respective homes. In fact, at this time I had no idea where Margaret lived, whether she was five miles away from me or five hundred. Shyly at first, we exchanged old footage of ourselves, of our childhoods and schooldays, our favorite foreign resorts.

Six months later we were married, at a lavish ceremony in the most exclusive of the studio chapels. Over two hundred guests attended, joining a huge hookup of television screens, and the service was conducted by a priest renowned for his mastery of the split-screen technique. Prerecorded films of Margaret and myself taken separately in our own sitting rooms were projected against a cathedral interior and showed us walking together down an immense aisle.

For our honeymoon we went to Venice. Happily we shared the panoramic views of the crowds in St. Mark's Square, and gazed at the Tintorettos in the Academy School. Our wedding night was a triumph of the director's art. As we lay in our respective beds (Margaret was in fact some thirty miles to the south of me, somewhere in a complex of vast highrises), I courted Margaret with a series of increasingly bold zooms, which she countered in a sweetly teasing way with her shy fades and wipes. As we undressed and exposed ourselves to each other the screen merged into a last oblivious close-up . . .

From the start we made a handsome couple, sharing all our interests, spending more time on the screen together than any couple we knew. Within due course, through AID, Karen was conceived and born, and soon after her second birthday in the residential crèche she was joined by David.

Seven further years followed of domestic bliss. During this period I had made an impressive reputation for myself as a pediatrician of advanced views by my championship of family life—this fundamental unit, as I described it, of intensive care. I repeatedly urged the installation of more cameras throughout the homes of family members, and provoked vigorous controversy when I suggested that families should bathe together, moved naked but without embarrassment around their respective bedrooms, and even that fathers should attend (though not in close-up) the births of their children.

It was during a pleasant family breakfast together that there occurred to me the extraordinary idea that was so dramatically to change our lives. I was looking at the image of Margaret on the screen, enjoying the beauty of the cosmetic mask she now wore—ever thicker and more elaborate as the years passed, it made her grow younger all the time. I relished the elegantly stylized way in which we now presented ourselves to each other—fortunately we had moved from the earnestness of Bergman and the more facile mannerisms of Fellini and Hitchcock to the classical serenity and wit of René Clair and Max Ophuls, though the children, with their love of the hand-held camera, still resembled so many budding Godards.

Recalling the abrupt way in which Margaret had first revealed herself to me, I realized that the logical extension of Margaret's frankness—on which, effectively, I had built my career—was that we should all meet together in person. Throughout my entire life, I reflected, I had never once seen, let alone touched, another human being. Whom better to begin with than my own wife and children?

Tentatively I raised the suggestion with Margaret, and I was delighted when she agreed.

"What an odd but marvelous idea! Why on earth has no one suggested it before?"

We decided instantly that the archaic interdiction against meeting another human being deserved simply to be ignored.

Unhappily, for reasons I failed to understand at the time, our first meeting was not a success. To avoid confusing the children, we deliberately restricted the first encounter to ourselves. I remember the days of anticipation as we made preparations for Margaret's journey—an elaborate undertaking, for people rarely traveled, except at the speed of the television signal.

An hour before she arrived I disconnected the complex security precautions that sealed my house from the world outside, the electronic alarm signals, steel grilles, and gas-tight doors.

At last the bell rang. Standing by the internal portcullis at the end of the entrance hall, I released the magnetic catches on the front door. A few seconds later the figure of a small, narrow-shouldered woman stepped into the hall. Although she was over twenty feet from me I could see her clearly, but I almost failed to realize that this was the wife to whom I had been married for ten years.

Neither of us was wearing make-up. Without its cosmetic mask Margaret's face seemed pasty and unhealthy, and the movements of her white hands were nervous and unsettled. I was struck by her advanced age and, above all, by her small size. For years I had known Margaret as a huge close-up on one or other of the large television screens in the house. Even in long-shot she was usually larger than this hunched and diminutive woman hovering at the end of the hall. It was difficult to believe that I had ever been excited by her empty breasts and narrow thighs.

Embarrassed by each other, we stood without speaking at opposite ends of the hall. I knew from her expression that Margaret was as surprised by my appearance as I was by her own. In addition, there was a curiously searching look in her eye, an element almost of hostility that I had never seen before.

Without thinking, I moved my hand to the latch of the portcullis. Already Margaret had stepped back into the doorway, as if nervous that I might seal her into the hall forever. Before I could speak, she had turned and fled.

When she had gone I carefully checked the locks on the front door. Around the entrance hung a faint and not altogether pleasant odour.

After this first abortive meeting Margaret and I returned to the happy peace of our married life. So relieved was I to see her on the screen that I could hardly believe our meeting had ever taken place. Neither of us referred to the disaster, and to the unpleasant emotions which our brief encounter had prompted.

During the next few days I reflected painfully on the experience. Far from bringing us together, the meeting had separated us. True closeness, I now knew, was television closeness—the intimacy of the zoom lens, the throat microphone, the close-up itself. On the television screen there were no body odours or strained breathing, no pupil contractions and facial reflexes, no mutual sizing up of emotions and advantage, no distrust and insecurity. Affection and compassion demanded distance. Only at a distance could one find that true closeness to another human being which, with grace, might transform itself into love.

Nevertheless, we inevitably arranged a second meeting. Why we did so I have still not understood, but both of us seemed to be impelled by those very motives of curiosity and distrust that I assumed we most feared. Calmly discussing everything with Margaret, I learned that she had felt the same distaste for me that I in turn had felt for her, the same obscure hostility.

We decided that we would bring the children to our next meeting, and that we would all wear make-up, modeling our behavior as closely as possible on our screen life together. Accordingly, three months later Margaret and myself, David and Karen, that unit of intensive care, came together for the first time in my sitting room.

Karen is stirring. She has rolled across the shaft of the broken standard lamp and her body faces me across the blood-stained carpet, as naked as when she stripped in front of me. This provocative act, presumably intended to jolt some incestuous fantasy buried in her father's mind, first set off the explosion of violence which has left us bloody and exhausted in the ruins of my sitting room. For all the wounds on her body, the bruises that disfigure her small breasts, she reminds me of Manet's Olympia, perhaps painted a few hours after the visit of some psychotic client.

Margaret, too, is watching her daughter. She sits forward, eying Karen with a gaze that is both possessive and menacing. Apart from a brief lunge at my testicles, she has ignored me. For some reason the two women have selected each other as their chief targets, just as David has vented almost all his hostility on me. I had not expected the scissors to be in his hand when I first slapped him. He is only a few feet from me now, ready to mount his last assault. For some reason he seemed particularly outraged by the display of teddy bears I had mounted so carefully for him, and shreds of these dismembered animals lie everywhere on the floor.

Fortunately I can breathe a little more freely now. I move my head to take in the ceiling camera and my fellow combatants. Together we present a grotesque aspect. The heavy television make-up we all decided to wear has dissolved into a set of bizarre Halloween masks.

All the same, we are at last together, and my affection for them overrides these small problems of mutual adjustment. As soon as they arrived, the bruise on my son's head and my wife's bleeding ears betrayed the evidence of some potentially lethal scuffle. I knew that it would be a testing time. But at least we are making a start, in our small way establishing the possibility of a new kind of family life.

Everyone is breathing more strongly, and the attack will clearly begin within a minute. I can see the bloody scissors in my son's hand, and remember the pain as he stabbed me. I brace myself against the settee, ready to kick his face. With my right arm I am probably strong enough to take on whoever survives the last confrontation between my wife and daughter. Smiling at them affectionately, rage thickening the blood in my throat, I am only aware of my feelings of unbounded love.

GINSBERG'S CHOICE

ANTLER · ANDY CLAUSEN · DAVID COPE · WALTER
FORDHAM · ROBERT MEYERS · MARC OLMSTED ·
RON RODRIGUEZ · MICHAEL SCHOLNICK ·
TOM SWARTZ

A selection of young poets edited and introduced by Allen Ginsberg

*Much true poetry in this late 70s decade's mail & Naropa's Kerouac
Poetics schoolroom, here's a condensed anthology of younger char-
acter chanced on—my recognition fixed on genius I could under-
stand, imagist-objectivist, based, as was my own development.
ANTLER age 30 Milwaukee bard, (City Lights will publish his
masterpiece* Factory) *exfoliates immense near-mathematic detailed
catalogues out of one-word concepts, a logic explored by Corso.
ANDY CLAUSEN aetat 28 noble suffering Whitmanic hod-carrier
Oakland Cal. inherited Neal Cassady's American energy transmis-
sion. DAVID COPE same age hid in Grand Rapids Mich. follows
the late Dr. Williams & his magnificent peer Reznikoff in practicing
direct treatment of phanopoeic world, his clarity solid as theirs, in-
credible tearful gift! WALTER FORDHAM slightly younger medi-
tates in Boulder Colo., meek sane housepainter recognizing in brief
flashes the nostalgic odd sensation of present space. ROBERT
MEYERS angel-faced apprentice printer at 21 master of naked
particularity and Pittsburgh soulful panorama. Visionary youths!
MARC OLMSTED also 21 inherited Burroughs' scientific nerve
& Kerouac's movie-minded line scattered on the page & nailed
down with gold eyebeam in San Francisco. RON RODRIGUEZ,
early 20s, first Kerouac Poetics School graduate came from D.C.*

with stentor voice & surreal understanding Carl Solomon & Philip Lamantia poetries, here sample his naïf-style extracultural prose poetry-dreams. MICHAEL SCHOLNICK, Wilkes-Barre original, drives cab Lower East Side N.Y., age 24 with beat optimist élan, activist Nuyorican & St. Marks's poesy clans. TOM SWARTZ anonymous workingman-teacher-perceiver mid-20s aged: I've collected his (& others') clear photos as models of poetic reality—raw mindfulness—the actual world in which it's possible to build more & more complex rhythmic & visionary poems.

—ALLEN GINSBERG, *February 1, 1978*

ANTLER: A POEM

LAST WORDS

As this girl lay asleep on the beach
An ant crawled up her nose and layed its eggs
And when they hatched and ate into her brain
She clawed away her face and died screaming.
Or that deep sea diver whose pressurized suit burst
Who was squeezed a liquid pulp of flesh
Up the air hose onto the deck,
A long strand of human spaghetti.
Or that man on a Japanese train killed by the severed leg
Of a suicide who jumped from a passing train,
A hundred miles an hour through his window.
Or Li Po launching himself like a paper boat toward the moon.
Or Aeschylus strolling along the shore
When an eagle, looking for a stone to crack a turtle's shell,
Spotted his pate gleaming in the sun.
Or that Pompeii boy immortalized in lava.
Or the unearthed coffin, the lid scratched and bloody inside.
Or abandoned by his family, the old Eskimo circled by wolves.
Or Superman no longer faster than a speeding bullet through
    his head.
Or Santa's helicopter crashing in a shopping center of expectant
    children.
Or six children trampled to death in Cairo by a mob
Rushing to a church where the Virgin had just appeared.

These deaths speak for themselves. They don't need last words.
As for me, I'm not looking into the sky for falling flower pots.
Yet any second sights of a rifle may fix on my brain.
Fourteen humans walked alive that day a perfect stranger
By the name of Whitman up in a tower of higher learning
Shot them down one by one. Just like that. Dead.
I think of that old man stoned by three children
    who jeered him out of his house.
If someone told me that's how I'd die in fifty years
I wouldn't believe it. Did anyone tell the old man?

How will I die? Cleaning a gun with my eyes?
Walking into a mirror? Driving into a tree to avoid a porcupine
    my learner's permit in my pocket?
I know the old philosophies. Yes, I've already died in a way.
My boyhood and all that. Showers of fingernails and hair.
The constant sloughing off of the cells of my body.
The death of all the semen that has left me.
My turds, moving to their own bewildered death.
Maybe it'll be like that first night in San Francisco
Waking up to go to the bathroom in Milwaukee,
And getting out of my old bed I walk into a new wall.
Maybe it'll be coming up or going down stairs in the dark
Thinking there's one more step when there isn't
Or not one more step when there is.
Will I choke on a bone, or be swallowed by a whale?
Or a death brimming with allusions—
Tugging a book from the tightly packed shelf
    I pull my whole bookcase over on me.
Or slow death: torture, cancer, leprosy, senility,
Or exotic: voodooed, cannibalized, human-sacrificed,
    devoured by man-eating plant.
Which is worse, being eaten alive or starving to death?
Dying crying for help or begging for mercy?
Yawning as the bomb drops in my mouth,
Sneezing in the avalanche zone,
Done in by hiccups that can't be stopped,
Or like in Stekel, that man who hid under the outhouse seat
And disemboweled his wife from beneath with a butcher knife.
    I look before sitting.
Or seeing my ultimate vision of absolute beauty

I scream as in horror comics—"AAARRRGGGHHH!!!"
Will I die laughing, be struck by lightning?
    Will I never know what hit me?
Maybe the sky will fall on me.
Maybe the ground'll just open up under me.
Maybe a gang of boys 'll pour gasoline over me and light me—
    or will it be a case of spontaneous combustion?
Will I be mistaken for a deer during deer season?
Or like Tita Piaz who climbed 9,000 feet of sheer rock 300 times
    with his son strapped to his back, only to die in a fall
    down his steps?
Or will one of the audience bump me off after the reading?

And when am I going to die? I'd like to know.
I don't want to get there when the show's half over.
I don't want to fall asleep. I'll have to poke myself.
I don't want to miss my death the way I missed my birth.
I sit here and plan my last words. I'm going to be prepared.
As in murder mysteries where the victim lies dying
And the hero holds him and says—"Who did it?"
In the same way they'll gather round me and ask—
    "What does this poem mean?"
    or "Do you really think *that* is beautiful?"
And then, like the murdered victim, I'll mumble far away
Feverishly trying to think of something profound and rising
    in pitch gasp
"It was It was It was It was . . ."
Then slumping back I die.

What will I say? Shall I make fart sounds with my lips?
Should I tell where the treasure's hidden?
Should I utter *Wanbli Galeshka wana ni he o who e?*
    My best friend's name?
Or make make-believe deathrattles better than birdlovers
    warble songs of their favorite birds?
Or should I join the chorus of thousands who shriek—"AAAIIIEEE!!!"
    or the thousands who simply go "O"
    or "Ugh" or "Oof" or "Whoops"
Or should I press finger to lips in the sign of silence?
Not content with ruling the world, Nero, wanting to be its supreme
    actor and musician, ordered full houses and awarded himself

all the prizes, and while he sang no one could leave,
though many pretended to die in order to be carried out
as corpses. Shall I say as he did when forced to commit
suicide—"What a great artist the world is losing!"
Or like Rabelais—"Bring down the curtain the farce is finished,"
and later as the priests surrounded him,
he, with a straight face, sighed—
"I go to seek a great perhaps."
Or like the Comtesse de Vercelles, according to Rousseau—
"In the agonies of death she broke wind loudly. 'Good!'
she said, "a woman who can fart is not yet dead.' "
Or like Saint Boniface as boiling lead was poured down his throat—
"I thank thee Lord Jesus, Son of the Living God!"
Or Saint Lawrence, broiled on a gridiron—"This side is done now,
turn me over."
Or Emily Dickinson—"I must go in, the fog is rising."
Or Beddoes—"I ought to have been among other things a good poet."
Or Lindsay, full of lysol—"They tried to get me . . . I got them
first."
Or Socrates—"Crito, I owe a cock to Asclepius,
will you remember to pay the debt?"
Or Chopin—"Swear to make them cut me open
so I won't be buried alive."
Or Scriabin, his face engulfed in gangrene—
"Suffering is necessary."
Or Marie Antoinette, having stepped on the executioner's foot—
"I beg your pardon."
Or Huey Long—"I wonder why he shot me?"
Or Millard Fillmore—"The nourishment is palatable."
Or P. T. Barnum—"How were the receipts today
in Madison Square Garden?"
Or Carl Panzarm, slayer of 23 persons—"I wish the whole human
race had one neck and I had my hands around it."
Or Jean Barre, 19, guillotined for mutilating a crucifix—
"I never thought they'd put a gentleman to death
for committing such a trifle."
Or da Vinci—"I have offended God and man
because my work wasn't good enough."
Or Vanzetti—"I am innocent."
Zeno, founder of the stoic school, striking the ground with
one fist—"I come, I come, why do you call for me?"

W. Palmer, stepping off the gallows—"Are you sure it's safe?"
Metchnikoff the bacteriologist—"Look in my intestines carefully
    for I think there is something there now."
John Wilkes Booth—"Tell my mother I died for my country."
Dylan Thomas—"I have had 18 straight whiskies. I think that's
    the record."
Dutch Schultz—"French-Canadian bean soup!"
Byron—"I want to go to sleep now."
Joyce—"Does nobody understand?"

Must I be the scribe of each word I speak,
    never knowing if it will be my last?
Or should someone else be my full-time scribe
    (in case deathfits keep me from writing them down)
Always ready to put ear to my lips
    in case it should be a whisper?
"Rosebud." "More weight." "More light."
"Now it is come." "Now I die." "So this is death?"
"Thank you." "Farewell!" "Hurrah!" "Boo!"
    "Can this last long?" "It is finished."
Or like H. G. Wells—"I'm all right. Go away."
Or like Sam Goldwyn—"I never thought I'd live to see the day."
Or like John Wolcott when asked if anything could be done
    for him—"Bring back my youth."

I tell myself what my last words will be,
Hoping I don't get stage fright.
Hoping I don't get laryngitis.
Hoping someone will hear them.
Hoping I'm not interrupted.
Hoping I don't forget what they are.
From now on everything I say and write
Are my last words.

ANDY CLAUSEN: THREE POEMS

1 THEY ARE COMING

I

There are many historical male poet derelicts
but the women all beautiful or well to do
    save the obscure few
but when the derelict women
    come for the laurel wreath
when the hag haired sots smile
       thru rotting mouths with atrophied wombs
       eructating abortions & other misfortunes
          this scene will change

II

They'll come from food stamp streets
    like everything wrong on television
they won't need know the clorox
    test for cocaine
or what myriad undulations of liberation
    mean to coeds masturbating at Bergman movies
They'll come with tired feet
    of concrete floors canneries & beaneries
They'll come with bleached eyes & blue lips
They'll come from lost children memories
    and pimped gone beauty
They'll come with dignity
They'll come like Mothers
The derelict women poets are coming!

2 THE STAR

A seasick man on sidewalk
    wobbled the 50 feet separating
    us on eye contact
"Where is the star?" he asks
"The what?"
"I need some food."

"You see these kids—another one inside—
        How did you old guys let the world
        get so fucked up?"
"I didn't do it," that wrinkled
        walnut, discard utters in tears which
        anchor him to concrete step
I tear into the kitchen
"Linda we got any food? There's some
wino out there cryin cuz he's hungry
        and I accused him of fuckin
        up the world— He said he didn't do it"
leftover cooked eggs
put between Muslim bread
wrap in cellophane—

"Here," I hand it to him
"Where's the Star?"
The Star? what crazy names
        they think of for these rescue missions
The Star? The Light!
You mean the Store!
Around the Corner—
Now he's smiling—
He'll make it—maybe—
if not—? what else is there?
do they have a dog pound for people?
What it is
is What it ain't
"The Star—corner," he grins
"Oh-da-lay," I say
He grins wider
"Oh-da-lay Puez"
My attempt at brotherhood
the magic words—
keep on keepin on
keep on truckin, right on bro, good luck
words words words
like broken glass on the sidewalk
        in the park in the gutter
Once I romanticized and blessed
        this broken glass

but as I see the barefoot children
I damned it forgiving the classless class
but Xavier said they are secret police—
They certainly are the jackoffs of society
Their minds ground up into Salami
     the priests disrobe for
Their faces relief maps of tortured planets
Their livers barely live
     clothes never fit
They have anarchy of the bowels
     and stink from everything
wandering
allowed streets & parks of poverty's children
the cement jumping up
     to attack them
in welfare mother laundromats
in alley ways in jails & morgues
I respect the Wino who makes it
     to the refuse container
     with his dead dog—
I forgive the she-whelped ones
     who don't
Who am I to forgive
     those who never forgive themselves?
     Well if Ford can pardon Nixon
     I can pardon them—
There is no way back
     for the unforgiven but forgiveness
Oh-da-lay, Oh-da-lay Puez—
Are they secret police?
Oh-da-lay, Oh-da-lay Puez—
these children in Death's clothing?

3
     We are not all figments
of our imaginations
     Tralalalala

DAVID COPE: TWO POEMS AND FRAGMENTS

CRASH

the cars lie, one on its side,
a rear wheel still spinning,
& the other upside down.
the bodies are scattered across the cornfield,
bent & broken on the frozen ground.
two ambulances pull up.
the attendants arrange & cover the dead.
cars pull over to the side of the road,
everyone shuffles,
eager to help, hands in pockets.

AMERICAN DREAM

the house was all in flames,
orange billows bursting up into the sunlight.
FBI agents & police were laid up
behind walls, sheds & other buildings,
armed with M-16s & rocket launchers.
the firemen were kept back.
the battle had gone on for some time
when the fire exploded thruout the house.
one of the bodies could be seen inside the house,
loaded with ammunition belts,
the bullets exploding from the heat.

FRAGMENTS FROM *THE STARS*

this is an AMERICAN POEM
accept no substitutes.
no surrealism or symbolism,
this is the asphalt under your feet.

·

an old woman leans against a tree
alone in the cemetery, the wind at her back.
now she turns back to her car,
the highway, home, coffee with friends.

•

lines of headlights extend to the horizon.
horns honking, flashing lights,
& overhead, the high thin poles
are silhouetted before the lavender sky.

•

the evening streets are full of ghosts
pleading for mercy.
sunset washes the windows red & they flash
over the river; the night comes on,
all sirens & bowling tournaments.

•

waiting for a bus
some laid-off workers shoot craps.
this one's won, he's dancing around
slapping at the losers.

•

two men are shouting outside the courtroom,
waving their arms, pointing to sheafs of paper
clutched in their fists.
police appear & escort them out, still shouting,
half dragged down the marble steps.

•

going to see friends
all the lights are out on the expressway.
a semi flies into our lane, not seeing us,
& we're skidding, slamming on the brakes.

WALTER FORDHAM: SEVEN POEMS

1 ALMOST WINTER

Rain on the black roof.
November. The hard lines
of black branches
on the gray sky.

Almost winter.
Makes me calm
with the year so old.
Work work work in the winter.
We have such easy lives.

2

In deep early morning darkness
with the earth stretching endlessly away
and sleep just gone for a moment:
the rain falling straight down
no light   no wind

3 APRIL

Crazy understanding in the morning
Last night I didn't want to be so happy
Every April when the warm rains come
I don't want to get so happy

4 BOSTON BUS STOP

Some people only want a ride home
others want each other
and a piece of flesh to hold.

All faces anxious regardless.
I want damp female
thighs to be lost in.

5
Wind in the maple tree
                no sun in the morning
no sense all day

6 GREASE COOK

Nine months working here
and not till this last
drunk night do I notice
the smell the fresh
bell peppers have
when I slice them fast

7 SITTING GIRL

She sees something here
that is not.
Eyes closed, palms up, naked
under blue print summer dress
she smiles into meditation hall
imaginary love light.

ROBERT MEYERS: TWO POEMS

STORM

What can one do
in the midst of thunderous hail
in the lightning flare arching cut
drum roar rain slick world
One cannot turn away in his house
it is too dynamic
the curl and cackle of sky pitch dark
steady ticking of rain, din of hail
Blue green electric illuminate
that for a split second
flashes on the colors of the world
green foliated hillsides
wet black roofs
The distant pinpricks of houses
wavering thru the storm
valley floor highway with cars
stalled close and confused in their path
confronted with heavy weather
No music on any media
can overbear the tempo of the storm
no duty or study cannot be pierced by it
The power surges over the atmosphere
quakes the house, beats the roof like a drum
windows vibrate with thunder booms
The violence reaches a crescendo
slacks, lulls, concedes again
goes off to the east
lightning winking over the next hill,
thunder rumbling like hunger.

Human sound, activity resumes
traffic hisses on wet highway
cars splashing water
Locomotives rush and cry
hunkering up the rivers side

In between fronts of cloud
wet earth scent of leaves wholesome
millsmoke sulfur drifts from south
In the midst from all windows
view the spark luminescent threads
the gathering and subsiding torrent
Sonorous on wood, tinny on glass
splatting on stone surface
gathering in pools, rushing off in jack streams current froth
Auras of water—beating down and raining upward
frieze of turbulences dance on ground

Storm passes, the world grows calm
to the sound of water gushing in gutters and streets
the hollowness prickly with humidity
the moistness dissipation affecting skin
the wearing of body temperature.

VIOLET

A yellow flower pale
        5 petaled
            faint lined purple vein tongue
            sensuous furze throated
            stems green leaves, heart shaped
                    gold inside.

MARC OLMSTED: TWO POEMS

1

        sodium pentothal gassed into
                    my arm
                the fag attendant
                    silver hair curling over

green smock whispers
"good night" and
the world goes out
grey machine
takes pictures of
my guts, white flash, a
lead sheet to prevent balls
going sterile
dye pumped hot
rush settling in
plexus-groin
a warm crawling, the
demerol giving transcendent
smiles, I'm dreaming this
acceptance of suffering
walk to the
bus stop slight fevered, sluggish
fulla weird chemicals
hospital awesome & cold two
blocks
down
a guy like Bela Lugosi next to me
where was I when existence
ceased on the operating table
meat dispossessed
and ugly without consciousness
strange beached fish
rubber mask vapor
of Uranus

2
I will swallow
all the pieces of myself
stone gong, vajra fallen
from the sky
science fiction instrument
I will swallow even thought
which is myself

        no skin of an idea
            will remain
        wind slams the door
            dead moths in the white
                snow dust, gold
                    light of window sill

RON RODRIGUEZ: FIVE POETRY DREAMS

LUNAR DESPAIR

I had just arrived to a newly built suburb in the moon, flat rectangular buildings scattered around a dry white rocky landscape, and was suffering a strange form of depression just lying around my house doing nothing especially since there was nothing to do on the moon. I decided to look for my former traveling companion, John D. but he was sent to a skid row that was just developed on the moon for former astronauts who had no more challenges in this world.

WALKING FISH

I was interrupted from watching a movie about the end of the earth by this character who brought in a bag full of walking fish and let them out on the aisle trying to peddle them off for $5 each. I felt very repulsed by the fish and stood up in order to avoid them. I begged the peddler to call them off but he wouldnt do it till I finally pulled a gun on him.

DEAD BODY

I was offered 5 grand to dispose of a guy who had o.d.'d in someone's apartment. I decided to drive the body to Connecticut while I kept it inside a laundrybag full of ice. My

car fucked up in New Jersey so I hitchhiked with the stiff up
to Connecticut but got stopped by the cops later on. They
asked me how come I wasn't working and what the hell I did
with my time but they didn't ask about the stiff. I got left off
in the middle of the New England Thruway on the way to
Rhode Island still trying to figure out how to dispose of the
body since I didn't have a car. I wondered if 5 grand was
worth all the trouble I was going through.

THE HOSPITAL

I was trying to find a hospital secluded by country roads. I got
as far as a dirt road thinking I had to walk but I found a kid's
wagon to ride on. Meanwhile some kids were taunting me
saying to each other, What is that nigger doing here? I got
down to a group of apartment buildings surrounded by a high
field of weeds. I walked up to the place, asked around for the
hospital, only to find out everybody was either taking a bath
or watching tv naked unaware of my presence.

IT MADE HIM LOOK LIKE A CONGRESSMAN

I had been inducted into the army and we were waiting for
the drill instructor to come around, I volunteered to look for
him outside the building which was in the middle of down-
town D.C. but they wouldn't trust me, then my father came
in with a mop over his head saying he would get me a job
and people believed him so I left and spent the rest of the day
walking around the stores with my father and him introducing
me saying I was looking for a job. We finally got home and I
asked my father why he had the mop on his head, he smiled
and said it made him look like a Congressman.

MICHAEL SCHOLNICK: TWO POEMS

FOR IRWIN HEILNER

Experience is disappointing,
that's why life's absurd.
I learned this watching you shave
lecturing about Beethoven
and prison reform
Polite man bathrobed
standing in your livingroom
I was company
". . . and all we can do," you said,
finger scanning neck cheeks
feeling baby red smooth skin,
"Is punish, punish, punish."
Now finding a hair then clipping
delicately
with a conductor's wrist

Wisdom flows in your speech
of an art to consciousness
heavier than Beethoven's fist
Amazing how he tamed such wildness
ordering blue soldiers in blue chariots
to march around the white Chinese teacup of his mind
How zapped with power he lifted his wrath
above the birds and clouds
above Napoleon's imagination
And smashed antiquity
dropping Quartets 14 15 & 16
on God's porcelain tongue

For you a musician
An eccentric librarian
whose deepest thoughts
dwell dusty and unpublished
The eternal is fierce and now
Who can deny your chilly chords?
For you scores of inspiration
Manuals cartons of sage sense

A humble universe
The science of your soul
in an unknown basement
on Dawson Avenue
in Clifton, New Jersey

CATSKILL SONG AND DANCE

When Hank Williams sings
    "Like a piece of driftwood on the sea
    May you never be alone with me"
I don't compare him to Shakespeare
I say "that's beautiful"
and play it again

What's in store for America?
Higher prices? Years of my poetry?
A renaissance of pretense and fascism?
The scholarship of shadows?
Love syndicated and blest
as uninspired businessmen consume the nation tolerating words?

I'm so glad to learn what spirit is
Now I'm not hungry
I'm a disciple peeling an orange
I'm he who sits on steps
watching the rain fall
After a while I'm back inside
thinking the same old thoughts

Solitary as a Russian novel
I hang my head in sorrow

Sorrow? I can't finish with sorrow
Not after Frank O'Hara
His selected self collected in my kitchen
Fast? Man he was fast
He was so fast he's dead

He was faster than a day or a shower
Faster than the Middle Ages and faster

At work
No one wants to take out the garbage
The waitresses just won't do it
and are allowed not to
They yell "Garbage" when the bag is full
And someone
Could be me
Steps out front

And when I step out the back door
And toss the dripping goods over the black rail
Into the green bin perfect!
I look around
And sometimes I can see the moon

TOM SWARTZ: FIVE POEMS

4/25/76 DAYLIGHT SAVINGS TIME

Sitting at home after
a long night
Mark and Joey stayed half an hour
Now they're gone
Our smoke's settled on
the leaves of the Ti plant
Electric clock hum

Finishing my newspaper route
red eyed in dawn light
over right shoulder
the Sunrise

6/19/76

A four wheel drift
around the corner
gravel stones unexpected
on asphalt
Turn right
        into skid
and turn back onto
manicured lawn missing
the black shadow of a
mailbox

Accelerator pushed
down to floor
gasoline fumes
filling the van
I toss my cigarette
out the window
and watch the red
sparks fly

A load of morning papers
and daybreak two
hours away
I adjust my speed to that
of the stoplights
Green!
I rush madly up one street and
down another
following the headlights

I am the midnight Angel
of the Boulder suburbs
At 3:00 A.M. even
stop signs have halos

8/19/76

Across the street/Apollo's
          taxi/sits
                    in a driveway
          meter running
I have seen yellow cabs
          bring in the morning
     parked beside a coffee shop
               (five A.M.
                    every third car
                              a cop)

POEM FOR MY TRUCK

Each winter you gain more rust
Spring washing reveals less paint
Though you contain the wisdom of Ford
Your rocker-panels 'll be gone in a year
You steer a bit to the right
My road all holes and dirt
Bald tread holds no stone
On payday I'll buy you new tires

THE WEATHERMAN'S APOLOGY

However   evaporation   moisture   cloud   drift
It rained on Florida   St. Petersburg
But not on the wind phantom white shirt
Not on the man in the grey car
A red pick-up one block ahead
Of the man in the grey car
Not on the Hotel Boulderado
Not where Japonica Way meets Juniper Street

A SINNER'S GUIDEBOOK

EDUARDO GUDIÑO KIEFFER

Translated from the Spanish by Ronald Christ and Gregory Kolovakos

She knows it, she knows she's the One and Only of Buenos Aires, *rara avis in terris;* she knows there's no other who can do what she does with the skill she does it; she knows she's the Phoenix, the Chosen One, the Incomparable, the heroic Joan of Arc, but no virgin, thank God;

she knows others exist, sure, she knows it because she herself belongs to that garrulous and multicolor fauna, because secret tropisms pushed her toward closed lodges, mysterious clans, guilds whose passwords are smirks, gasps, and sashaying;

she knows others exist but few of them dare to wear the bracelets, necklaces, beads, plumes, high heels, and fake eyelashes except in clandestine mystical phallic ceremonies while she, the One and Only, can strut all that in public, in front of rows and rows of seats packed with hot bodies with lascivious or jeering eyes; the All Defiant, the All Enlightened and not because of some miraculous Celestial Charity but because of Violet Spots describing a center-stage halo at the Orléans; guided not by Voices but by the Sublime Electronic Music;

and she also knows she has almost or completely magical powers; she knows how that audience shouts obscenities at Leila (Rita Fuad in real life) while she takes off her veils to the tune of "In a Persian Market"; they stamp and whistle while Yoko (Yolanda Cardoza in real life) takes off her kimono to "Poor Butterfly"; they get worked up to fever pitch while Marilyn (Rosita Kluczinsky in real life) takes off her tight-fitting black dress to "Blues in the Night"; but

61

they grow quiet, surprised at first, and then absolutely fascinated, stupefied, bewitched, wrapping her in an almost frightening silence when the esoteric violet aura is switched on and the choral prelude "Jesu, Joy of Man's Desiring" starts up unexpectedly, solemnly, strangely, anagogically;

that's when she comes out of the shadows to station herself under the lights, in her snow-white, floor-length tunic and her jewels like scapulars, like medallions, and her fluttering false silky eyelashes and her ceremonial high heels and the languid wig; she comes forward and hardly begins to move to the contemplative phrasing of the chords;

first raise the right arm then the left in immolation and holocaust let the hair fall forward covering the face bending the head slowly push out the hip advance the leg letting the taut muscle be seen through the furtive slit, oh anointed priestess in the androlatrous ritual of her own adoration, first take off the earrings then the neck-laces then the bracelets then one shoe then the other to the beat of the holy sacrifice, and the crowd's silence getting denser moment by moment and the music more overwhelming moment by moment essentially more and more Bach moment by moment interpreted by Walter Carlos on the Moog neosynthesizer and toward the end of the two minutes and fifty-seven seconds which is exactly how long the number lasts let the white tunic drop dramatically turn away from the audience unsnap the bra turn around again facing the thousand-headed monster silenced transported hypnotized modestly covering the breasts with both arms and now without uncovering it with one arm lower the other slllooowllly slloowlly until loosening the small rose on the panties and then with a properly miraculous precision "Jesu, Joy of Man's Desiring" ends and the spots go off and the violet halo is extinguished and the darkness covers her total nudity with mourning clothes and crepe and she runs off between the teasers and quickly puts on the raincoat she left hanging there on a nail just for that purpose;

she also knows that during those two seconds after the lights go out, those two clocked seconds, silence will reign over the orchestra of the Orléans like smoke from the cigarettes, like the echo of that already faded music; and then someone will clap and applause from those who have realized for the very first time that strip tease can be something like a solemn mass, a votive mass, a mass of purifica-tion with the body present;

she also knows (although she'd like to forget it) that the applause would roar out of a maddened beast if the light didn't go out at exactly the right moment and if the public discovered the truth, that deceitful truth or, better said, that painful reality she feels between her legs while walking toward the dressing room, oh God, dear God of my soul how mean you were to me when you put this right here, what do I want with something so lovely on men so useless on me, why do you make me feel more of a woman than any woman and you stuck a prick where I'd like to have something else, warm and loving;

sure, the applause would roar out and she would die, crushed by the cheated furious irate iconoclastic crowd and maybe it would be beautiful to die like that with all those sweaty drunken ferocious men on top, stepping on her, spitting on her, and tearing at her;

but the lights always go out on time and she goes to the dressing room (the girls, her associates, say "changing room," but she prefers to say dressing room, it's so much more elegant, so much more aristocratic, dressing room instead of changing room, maybe Sarah Bernhardt had a changing room, no, surely she had a dressing room, maybe Maria Callas has a changing room, but enough of that);

and in the dressing room the noisy chatterboxes talking complaining it's disgraceful three thousand pesos a day and on my last tour of Central America I was earning a thousand dollars a month; shut up what're you talking about Central America for if you never made it past Berazategui; it's easy to see you're blabbing out of jealousy, what's happening is if you keep getting fatter you're not going to be able to strip any more, who's going to pay to see cellulitis, and the laughing and the nasty cracks and did'ja get a load of that and, but what a thing to say;

and when she enters and sits down in front of the mirror and begins to take off her makeup with Aqualane even though Aqualane is used for other necessities, there's a very short silence having nothing to do with the great majestic silence in the theater; a short silence caused by the fact that the others, even doing what she is doing, would love to feel as feminine as she does;

and while she makes the blush and rouge and shadow disappear with a slow and circular massaging of her fingertips on her forehead, on her cheeks, on her neck, the others watch waiting for that ridiculous and sublime moment that is repeated like a sacrament every night;

that moment she waits for too, a martyr facing the lions, a sacrificial victim;

that moment which should also have some background music because it is the moment of true nudity, awesome solemn Wagnerian music that would make the last interior masks fall away:

THE MOMENT OF TAKING OFF THE WIG

now,

like this;

and what is it as if they don't know by heart, as if I haven't repeated it every night these last three years;

take it off suddenly, with a quick jerk, in a defiant gesture that exposes her skull where two or three stray hairs do not cover the miserable premature baldness, sign of a masculinity unchosen but inevitable;

that moment;

she with the wig in her hand looking at the others with a blank stare, the others lowering their eyes as if ashamed suddenly breaking the silence with small talk, something about the weather or about the fat man in the front row, anything;

and little by little the return to normality, she taking off the false eyelashes now with Johnson's Baby Oil, as good for her very delicate eyelids as for very delicate babies' rear ends; the others beginning to ask her things and she replying as if she were the lonely-hearts column, answering Yoko (Yolanda Cardoza in real life) who consults her about whether it's worthwhile to give up the Orléans and devote herself to studying anthropology, or listening to the moaning of Leila (Rita Fuad in real life) who complains that men are all the same or ducking the innuendos of Marilyn (Rosita Kluczinsky in real life) who attacks her because she's envious, of course;

but the one sure thing is that when all is said and done they all depend on her, all revolve around her, the One and Only of Buenos Aires, *rara avis in terris,* Phoenix, Joan of Arc;

the One and Only capable of imagining that it's possible to strip to Bach put to electronic music;

the One and Only capable of dominating that dragon audience;

the One and Only whose sex is a false sex and yet more genuine than the female bearers of a genuine sex;

the only One and Only;

Corybant at the mad feast of Cybele, druid in the forest of sky-scrapers, hierophant officiating at secret ceremonies;

Pope Joan on a canopied throne but on the pyre every day as

well, on the sacrificial altar ready to receive a dagger in the center
of her breast;

the only One and Only;

who's now entirely clean of makeup, entirely divested of wig,
high heels, and false eyelashes, who now stands up, letting the rain-
coat slip off, who with perfect naturalness walks naked in front of
the others who don't even look at her because they're so used to her
by now, who walks trying to move her skimpy buns as if they were
the mighty buttocks of the others, showing off what she doesn't
have and embarrassing herself with what she does have, oh God my
God how mean you were to me;

heading toward the locker where the striped pants pink shirt
sandals are that she'll wear on the street because obviously, on the
street you can't dress like a woman even if you'd like to;

listening to the little cries of the others the goodbyes of the others
who and, dressed now, watching them with her head thrown back
and the right eyebrow disdainfully raised like Maria Felix as an
Aztec deity, sweeping them with a circular gaze, a fiery gaze that
could incinerate these other poor women for more than being just
that: women;

and flinging a half languid, half scornful ciao that drops in the
midst of Leila, Yoko, and Marilyn like a wilted carnation that tears
out the other carnations, other flowers other ciao sweetheart see you
tomorrow, good luck, hope something turns up, hope everything
goes well, see ya', good night;

and going out on to the street and crossing over to the bar to dial
a number on the payphone;

beep beeep beep beep busy;

then sitting down at the usual table asking Mario for the usual
Mario coffee please

Mario attentive bringing her the coffee asking how're you how're
things going;

sweetheart, things are always pretty good, justa little tired, you
know, when a lady's an artist;

a startled customer who turns around hearing the hoarse voice
refer to herself in the feminine gender, when the voice as well as
the appearance indicate the masculine;

she winking an accomplice eye at Mario and another devilish eye
at the customer and the customer turning red up to here and bury-
ing himself in the pages of *La Razón* and Mario's accomplice smile;

the hot coffee does her good, stimulates her stomach, awakens the the gratifying memory of her strip tease, the only number of the One and Only, others would've liked to have had the idea, but what were they going to do, so few like classical music, so few who'd think of using Bach for the art of stripping in public;

ten minutes and to the telephone again, once again to dial the number engraved in her memory and now, yes, ringing, one, two, three, then the click and his sleepy voice:

hello who 's it;

and she the only One and Only suddenly quaking shivering timid trembling Joan of Arc defeated, handed over letting herself be condemned, yearning for the burning flames, pronouncing just one word:

love;

oh, it's you;

love, tell me that you love me;

shit, you want to be flattered at this hour;

I'm done now, I'm coming out there, I want to see you, please let me in don't be mean;

look, you nut, I'm really tired;

please, sweetheart;

go fuck yourself;

oh cruel stab, oh another click from him when he hangs up, oh injustice, oh pain, oh broken heart;

suddenly wilted, humiliated, repentant, hurt alone

paying for the coffee while Mario looks on sympathetically

going out on to the street alone

walking to the bus stop alone

getting on the bus alone

riding alone

getting off the bus alone

entering her two-room apartment in the Abasto, right there on Gardel Street alone;

looking at the photo of Manfredi under the glass on the bedside table alone;

getting ready for bed alone;

looking at herself in the mirror, seeing herself alone;

alone alone so alone,

and to top it off bald.

SEVEN PROSE POEMS

JEAN COCTEAU

Translated from the French by Perry Oldham

WONDERS OF NATURE

Dazed by the sun. The blow wears off and the turning causes
a swarm of decals to leave the hat. The thistle is a window-
pane shattered into a thousand splinters. The bear hunter
easily captures the bear by grabbing the ring in its nose. One
catches butterflies with a book of pictures. The dust damages
them greatly. On rainy days, one shuts oneself up and plays
with blocks. If the sun is shining, one goes for a walk and
overripe colors embellish the game of blocks. On this side, one
sees a mountain landscape. The other five sides combine the
sea, the house, the lake, the forest, the town.

It is a chance to be above it. The rest takes place in secret.

GRAVITY OF THE HEART

Water flows in the fountains, grave as the mouth of a dog. A
rose intimidates me; it never laughs. And the tree sleeps
standing. It never makes jokes. For example, it commands its
shade: lie down, rest, we set off again this evening. In the eve-
ning the shadow climbs up into the branches, and they leave
once again.

One who is in love writes on the walls.

If I were to look upon my heart, I would no longer dare to smile at you. It labors so hard in this moonless night. Lying upon you, I await its gallop which brings me bad news.

THE ENCHANTED MEERSCHAUM LOAF OF BREAD

The red glove of crime   The serpent's train   Its head which is a revolver   Gangrene   The young sailor who pastes on a stamp   Ace of clubs   Oh!   my God! what will become of his thumb?   it is condemned to death Venus, all in rose, sitting in a thousand carriages smashed against the wall   Mint, cornflower, drum, grenadine And the enchanted loaf of bread which flies away over the roof.

BLUE BEAUTY

The sky's opening said Ah! in fireworks heart parachutes blue mouth open one sees through the starry sky to the back of its throat and if it says Ah! and Oh! all of God falls slowly like a curtain at the Opéra.

THE BLUE ANCHOR

Judicial error was induced by the words "anchor" and "ink." In reality the sailor was waiting for a letter written, not in blue ink, but at *THE BLUE ANCHOR*, a waterfront bar. Through fatal ill luck, after the crime, the police collected, near the collar of the French sailor's pea jacket, an American sailor's fountain pen, filled with blue ink. It is admissible,

then, that the sailor, but which one? being asleep with the
light on, the woman, eye glued to the keyhole, saw, from the
corridor, on the shoulder or rather on the surface of the shoul-
der having the capricious form of the keyhole, an anchor of
that magical blue employed by Chinese tattooers and easily
confounded with Waterman ink.

THE BUST

One simply has to consider it, that is all. To resolve the prob-
lem requires a certain acquaintance with the mysterious prop-
erties of marble. In brief, here is how the Roman bust pro-
ceded.

It waited for black night. Then, unfolding the noose whose
sinuosity, not forgetting that of sockets, of the superciliary
arch, of nostrils, ears and lips, formed innumerable shapes,
unfolding, I tell you, methodically, longer than a river, more
solid than steel, suppler than silk, this living thing able to go
into a spin, pierce walls, slip underneath doors and through
keyholes, attentive (without losing sight of the task) to the
least knots which it untied and then had to do up again under
pain of death, the ingenious and cruel bust, after passing
through several nocturnal chambers, strangled the sleeping
man.

THE RED PARCEL

My blood has turned to ink. It was necessary to prevent this
disgusting occurrence at all costs. I am poisoned to the bone.
I was singing in the night and now it is this song which
frightens me. Better yet: I am leprous. You know those spots
of mildew like a profile? I do not know which of my leper's
charms deceives the world and authorizes it to humiliate me.
So much the worse for it! Consequences do not concern me.
I have never exhibited anything but sores. They speak of
graceful fantasy: it's my fault. It is foolish to exhibit oneself
needlessly.

My disorders are piled to the sky. Those that I loved were tied to the sky with a rubber band. I turned my head . . . they were no longer there.

In the morning I bend over, I bend over and let myself drop. I am dropping from fatigue, from sorrow, from sleep. I am frazzled, nothing. I know no numbers, no dates, no names of rivers, no tongues, living or dead. I am a zero in history and geography. It is a miracle I'm not hunted. What's more I have stolen the papers of a certain J. C. born at M. L. le . . . , dead at 18 after a brilliant poetic career.

This head of hair, this poorly situated nervous system, this France, this land, are not mine. They disgust me. I rid myself of them at night in dream.

I have loosened the parcel. Let them shut me up, let them lynch me. Comprehend if you can: *I am a lie that always speaks the truth.*

SIX POEMS

ANDRÉ DU BOUCHET

Translated from the French by Cid Corman

TRANSLATOR'S NOTE. *André du Bouchet—born 1924 (my exact coeval)—has translated much work from English—Joyce and Shakespeare included—has written on artists like Giacometti and Tal Coat (who are or were close friends)—has been a seminal figure—in his own quiet way—in the French poetry scene during the past twenty-five years. He was a friend and translator also of Paul Celan (who—in turn—translated some of his work). His chief poetry collections have been (many have appeared in smaller art editions)* Dans la Chaleur Vacante *and* Ou le Soleil *(both by Mercure de France) and* Laisses. *His work has been featured in* Origin *3rd series and again in the current 4th series. He lives in Paris.*

SHUTTERS

The woman going to the window, so high in the house, up near the sun, draws the curtains, slowly lowers the white blind, and the window's effaced. In native gold. Bird's eye.

The make of the room restored, iron age, on the downstairs floor, behind the eye's white fleck.

HIGH SEAS

Head horizontal
the knee
cut by the light's white thread

the casements and branches confuse in
the screen

day picks up the needle
bosom
room of waves

EFFIGY

Wicks
and this eye that advances step by step

I walk in an eye that I do not know

these dull words
these flashes of light I do not understand

the worn earth

perhaps I've lacked patience

head sinks
already.

I SEE ALMOST NOTHING

The paper I cut
is wet
the mountain is almost concealed by its white surplice

the words grow calm
and regain
their position

the air hotter than the skin

I go out at last

it isnt me who cuts these streets

all exists so firm
and still
I cannot let go my hand

outside

I seem almost nothing.

THE SECOND SCYTHE

Once more further than the wind. But without leaving the
day. O undeluded, O you who lean on the heat of the ex-
panse!

STATION

Day,
house at the edge of the first
road. And that cold look burning on our face,

the face of summer.

It isnt we who go, it's the
fire that goes.
Summer,
perhaps,
which enters
in broad daylight the main room, like a cloud
moving above whitened façades.

MARRIAGE

W. J. HOLINGER

My marriage is five years old. Last night my wife dreamed of Karl-Otto. Karl-Otto was her German lover. Their relationship was intense, and it was not brief. It is over now except that it lingers in her mind, it lives in her imagination (and perhaps, also, in Karl-Otto's). The eighteen-month affair occurred two years before I met my wife; yet now it threatens me.

My marriage is controlled by my wife. If I tried to control it (I have no desire to control it), conflict would develop, and my wife would probably leave me. She did not marry me seeking conflict. She is very beautiful, very capable: very strong. If she were indecisive and unclear, as I am, perhaps neither of us would control this marriage. Then it might change from day to day, deteriorating for a while, then improving—who knows?

But Gwendolen, my wife, seems to know what she wants from our marriage, how she wants it to go. She controls the marriage by remaining conscious of what her goals are, and by controlling me through my emotions.

I have a crush on my wife, I am *in love* with her; I am dependent upon her; I love her more than I am loved by her. I respond to her behavior: to her touch, her tone of voice, her facial expression. During our five years of marriage Gwendolen has learned the nature of my various emotional responses, and how to elicit those she favors. I have few surprises left for her; I sense that she has stopped looking for them.

Since I have known Gwendolen she has borne no children. Once when she and Karl-Otto were making love, Gwendolen has told me, she cried out in a fit of ecstasy and longing.

"I want to have your baby!" she cried. It seemed to be something she wanted very badly to say, though she still isn't sure why.

Karl-Otto already had three daughters, however, and he was married to somebody else. He was thorough in his precautions against impregnating Gwendolen, who has told me that if she cannot have children by Karl-Otto, she does not want children at all.

That's all right with me. (Children are always hungry and always so busy.) I have no idea what either of us would do with a child.

I recently asked my wife why she had married me.

"To pass the time," she replied.

For me, the time does not pass quickly. My only respite is my work, which I find stimulating. I do only free-lance work. My office is in our home. There are days when, were my work not so engrossing, I would surely find existence unbearable.

Gwendolen is a laboratory assistant at a prestigious university. Having acquired difficult skills in Bremen (other than those taught her by Karl-Otto), she is a highly specialized technician. Her salary is substantial and she can choose her own hours. She comes and goes seemingly at random. She will quit the house with no warning, capriciously; she returns whenever she pleases—or according to some other motivating factor, the nature of which she doesn't disclose and I cannot discern.

Thus, always, I am either anticipating a sudden, unexpected, and unsettling departure, or awaiting with anxiety her return.

For me, then, time does not flow—it grinds, friction being caused by anticipation: my state of mind the chalkboard, and time the rasping fingernail.

What role do I take in our marriage?

I am the *hausfrau*. My job—or my lack of one—allows me the time. I prepare the meals, and I clean the house. Gwendolen's erratic hours and impulsive departures prevent her from responsibly performing these recurrent tasks.

Another role: sexually, I am the aggressor. That is the way

Gwendolen would have it, and often, after a sexual encounter, she compliments me.

I am always completely content, sexually drained. Gwendolen has never failed to satisfy me.

Karl-Otto, she says, was even more aggressive than I, more bold: original, gymnastic, insatiable. I point out that he was younger than I am now, and so was she. She doesn't argue the point. She smiles, and turns away.

My wife's fantasies are of greater import to her than reality. That is, she values her own inner life more than she does others' perceptions of how she acts. Occasionally other people's reactions to her do slightly influence her inner life (her dreams, her emotions); but people's opinions of my wife seldom have any influence upon her at all.

I do not know whether I play a role in any of my wife's fantasies.

She has indicated, however, that when she knew Karl-Otto, what he thought mattered a great deal to her, and what they did was practically everything to her. When she was with him, her inner and her outer lives were as one.

For Gwendolen, the past is more real, more valid than the present. She has photographs, notes, and memorabilia to refer to. Included in her collection of date books, ticket stubs, and other mementos is an aluminum-foil package, with German lettering, in which was once wrapped a prophylactic of sheepskin. The package appears to have been torn open hastily.

These things seem to authenticate for Gwendolen her memories. She searches them periodically. The photographs and objects of significance endure; through them her memories are renewed; and so the events themselves become a lingering experience, carried through time as tangible reality.

But she can only carry so much, and the present—her life with me—for the most part lies unnoticed as she passes by.

Have you ever felt that you wanted to stop time? That in the present moment you are fulfilled, and you would like to end your journey through life right there: freeze the moment, and stay forever?

Gwendolen, in some ways, has been able to.

She has two images of herself: those of the photographs, and that of the mirror. She prefers the former, the photographs. "Snaps," she calls them.

"Isn't this a wonderful snap?"

The *snap* of frozen time. I can hear the shutter—*snap!*—and a part of my wife remains there.

Occasionally I remind her that she cannot go back. "I don't have to," she replies, gazing at me.

Karl-Otto has a long nose—angular, sharply defined. On another man's face it might have come to serve as the focus of scorn and ridicule. Not so on Karl-Otto's. It fits right in with the sardonic expression he wears in most of Gwendolen's photographs. His carriage and physique are quite consistent with that nose. He does not just wear it; he *brandishes* it.

He has jet-black hair; the eyes are clear, full of life—self-assured and mocking. He seems to convey a sense of irony, a self-conscious awareness of the camera's reach and power—of his role in the photograph and in my wife's then-future life. As if, then, he was conscious of his image's effect now.

Full of youthful strength and confidence, he grins out at me from those photos and dares me to interfere with his cuckolding, challenges me to revenge myself.

A fantasy of mine, from which I receive considerable release and pleasure, is imagining various ways in which I would destroy those photographs of Gwendolen's. I see a widening flame rise from the match I hold, blackening and curling the photograph. Karl-Otto's face actually registers shock, agony, as his body is charred black from bottom to top.

But upon the surface of the curled black remnant is left an afterimage, a white silhouette of the static bodies and furniture of the photograph. A further reminder. There is light rustling as I grind the ashen flake to powder.

And I know also that, inadvertently, unavoidably, I would destroy Gwendolen too, who was there with Karl-Otto.

I too have memories. Many of them—the best ones—are of Gwendolen. She is a tender, erotic female in these memories, many of which involve sex.

Gwendolen was the first woman I ever seduced. Not that I had had no sexual experience; I'd had a good deal. But my experience was all with women greatly attracted to me, or with prostitutes, and Gwendolen was neither. She was beautiful, extremely desirable —but indifferent. Uninterested. I wanted her desperately—I had never really wanted such a grand woman before, I was helpless— and so I planned carefully, and one evening, in the most rational and premeditated manner, I set about seducing her. Aperitifs, a pork sauerbraten, fried potato cakes and ratatouille, Rhine wine, candles, music, Cointreau following the meal . . .

I succeeded. For the first time I reveled in exposing that magnificent woman: down fell her hair (her neck smelled of lilacs), her shoulders a creamy yellow in the candlelight, stockings drifting gently to the floor, the zipper's buzz, the rustle of her dress . . . Her skin was soft, delicate; her breath smelled faintly of garlic.

In the living room, on the floor (a deep rug, my silk-lined suit jacket beneath her), her lips trembled and a feline purr arose in her throat: "Oh Karl," she breathed, "oh Karl Karl Karl . . ."

I have encouraged Gwendolen to tell me stories of her life with Karl-Otto in Bremen eight years ago. She enjoys the experience; and though her enjoyment gives me some pleasure, I find listening to her stories to be interesting but disturbing.

It is my hope, however, that sharing the stories will provide Gwendolen and me a mutual realm of association, a solid base of common memory—as shared experience has not done for us.

The stories become quite intricate. Abridgement is necessary. Karl-Otto's secretary, a capable, lonely, middle-aged woman, came to resent Gwendolen with extreme passion. It was not Karl-Otto's infidelity toward his wife, but his infidelity toward herself which offended her, for she was desperately in love with Karl-Otto. Though aware of her feelings toward him, Karl-Otto took no notice of them, but rather maintained a discreetly professional, impersonal relationship with her.

As Trudy (Karl-Otto's secretary) gradually became aware of her employer's developing affair (Gwendolen often phoned him at his office, and occasionally met him there), her hatred of Gwendolen festered until an overt manifestation of it was unavoidable. Gwendolen had increasing difficulty telephoning Karl-Otto at his office (Trudy, of course, handled all incoming calls). When she did put Gwendolen through she often listened in; eventually (knowing their plans) she began to follow my wife and Karl-Otto when they went off together at noon or in the evening. Before too long,

Gwendolen tells me, she and Karl-Otto became aware of Trudy's behavior, and began first to expect her and to look for her, and later to lead her on. It developed into a diverting game. They spiced up their phone conversations; they became more and more intimate in public (here I press Gwendolen for details; she continues without elucidating); clandestinely they took photographs of Trudy lurking in hotel lobbies, or desperately seeking them in the noonday rush of Bremen. And yet, by means of invented codes and prearranged signals, they managed a private rendezvous whenever they wanted one.

The knowledge that someone spied on them, eavesdropped and shadowed them—the feeling that it mattered immensely to someone else—served to greatly enhance the affair for Gwendolen and Karl-Otto.

Trudy took none of it lightly. She played the game with deadly seriousness. She pursued them to all corners of Bremen, and it became very involved for Karl-Otto, who had his wife to think about as well.

Karl-Otto fired Trudy; but that did not get rid of her. She continued to shadow them, and she wrote notes to Karl-Otto threatening to expose him to his wife. Finally she was seen carrying a camera with a telephoto lens.

It was at this point that Karl-Otto felt he had to choose. He chose his marriage, his wife and three children, the stability (everything is relative) of their home: he abandoned Gwendolen.

Gwendolen left Bremen. "I don't like leaving," she has told me. "I never want to leave anywhere again."

And yet she leaves me all the time. And, really, she's never left Karl-Otto. He is with her still.

I am leaving my wife.

It is not the only thing I might do, but it is the right thing.

By leaving her I become a memory to her, I shall begin to live in her imagination—I shall become important to her.

I have some snaps of us which I can send her, a few at a time. I have tape recordings, the existence of which she cannot suspect. I have spliced and joined calendars so that they depict the days Gwendolen and I were together. I shall mail them to her, and a clock, too: a clock with frozen hands.

And what am I left with? For me it is not nearly so devastating as you might imagine. Quite the opposite: at last I can cease to long for her. I know Gwendolen well (the images are clear); I can predict how she will respond to my actions. I can anticipate her responses to my leaving, to my packages, and to her memory of me. I can imagine her fantasies.

Her inner life will become my inner life. I will be happy.

FOUR POEMS

GAVIN EWART

THE LEGEND

Well, there was this group called Spunky Sandwich,
they were friends of an eccentric called Monotype Bembo—
and he cured the lead guitarist of an incurable disease
(which reminds me that I once had a friend, a very witty man,
who said that another friend's wife was an incurable diseuse,
because she never stopped talking), and so they all lived
in a state of Karma or Grace or something,
and that summer, I remember, there was a plague of ladybirds
which are somehow connected with the Virgin Mary
(and the name, I suppose, invokes Our Lady),
they were all over everything and would even bite you.

And it wasn't as if Joseph of Arimathea's thorn tree
was blazing away, there weren't any mystical properties.
They were living together in the house of a woman
who was called Bossy Batches, a perfect rhombus,
very strict about dusting but not very pious,
and Monotype just stood up one morning at breakfast
(they were eating Mrs. Horsfield's Rough Cut Marmalade)
and invoked the First Cause and afterwards, simply,
blessed the lead guitarist's corn flakes;
and at once he lost his cancer (I think it was the rectum)
and his withered arm assumed its proper proportions.

I'm an old man now and my mind goes wandering,
counting sheep and wool-gathering, all these expressions
have to do with dreaming and trancelike sleep-states,
as I sit here in my corner, my pipe a baby's dummy
keeping me happy in my second childhood.
Some people have told me I *look* like a sheep
but I'm not very worried, after all the Lamb of God
may or may not have nibbled these pastures.
Miracles are commonplace, history is full of them;
this one had its time and its place. I just tell you
the circumstances as far as my mind lets me remember.

AN EXHIBITION OF LEONARDO DA VINCI'S ANATOMICAL DRAWINGS

Down the side and around
each physiological fragment
the looking-glass text is spread,

back to front, secretive,
with the downstrokes suggesting a spider.
Science the interest then—

but now they are students of art
who admire; there are medical textbooks,
no medical students are here.

Though aridities known to the lab,
like "The bones of the foot and dissections
of the neck" feature here on the page,

there is one where the students all stop:
"Coition of the hemisected
man and woman." They stand,

something that touches us most,
their backbones and organs in section
so beautifully drawn, but all cold;

the supply of emotion's from us—
who know how the power of this instinct
is expert at rocking the boat.

Passion is far from what's drawn,
there's a half-hearted curve in the penis,
she has an old woman's dugs.

They fit together all right,
but so mechanistic and static.
In my mind I go back to the days

when, sixteen, at a prim public school
I first read about Leonardo.
"Coitus," he seemingly wrote,

"is so disgusting that if
there were no pretty faces, if custom
and man's sensuality should

not condone it, the race would die out."
And Freud of course had his theory,
based on the bird/oral dream.

I note an obsession with hands.
They recur, in the drawings, in profusion.
But we must admit that this man,

with his genius near to a god,
was an atheist left-handed fairy.
Let prude philistines ponder on that.

KENILWORTH COURT

I couldn't write a hymn to that tremendous erection
in brash ithyphallic (in trochaic dimeters, brachycatalectic)
but there, just as much as Everest, it is;
with each block dated, 1901 to 1905,

in a sort of striated pink and brown—
the style Osbert Lancaster once called Pont Street Dutch.

Victoria was still alive when they started building,
I like to think, the first block. So it called from the swamps
    of time
its fellow mastodons—in the name of Edward.
This is the most solid and lasting
of all English domestic architecture.
They cluster round, on three sides, identical quintuplets.

The first owners must have had servants. Just imagine!
Prim maids in uniforms and solemn gentlemen's gentlemen—
even perhaps butlers. Who can tell?
Up until the Twenties, I should guess,
with its Bright Young Things and Oxford hearties
who, as a sex-mad French cad, would have debagged Debussy.

And the air over these mild domestic battlements floated
just as indifferently then (which now constitutes a flight path,
the pterodactyls are back, eager to tease
the sleeping monsters, dinosaurs of brick)
as through an Abdication and two World Wars
it held its neutrality, aloof beneath all the bombers.

Some day they'll smash these walls, brick from brick, the brutal
end of what could never be called an Ancient Monument—
the Putney Hippodrome's already gone
(it wasn't, truly, very pretty).
Time is like the atmosphere, it floats over us
invisible. But it does things. Poisongaslike, we see the effects
    of its passing.

SONNET: WHAT WE ARE

If you think of us one way, we're all huge sexual organs
walking about the world; so much of our physical
(let alone our psychological) nature
is devoted to attracting a mate, to reproduction.

The curves of the cheeks, the smallness of waists, the breadth
    of the shoulders
are all signals sent out on behalf of the Life Force.
Even (or especially) pornography recognizes this
in those films that feature (as they do): King Cock, Queen Cunt.

All creatures that reproduce in other ways
are something else again. Even the stiff praying mantis,
who squares up to her mate like a boxer
and eats him, is more akin to us than
the organisms that do not have two sexes.
Puritans are silly. They deny their essence.

EIGHT POEMS

from *Glyphs*

PAUL PINES

1
They're moving the fixtures out of THAU'S.

They're carrying out the stool
on which Edith-of-the-Swollen-Feet
sat nursing her edema.

Where the stove had been,
against the wall,
a heavy plaque of grease.

Max says:

—Hey, Paul, you want the mirrors,
or a piece of the counter?

This is how it ends:
52 years of food encrustation,
and intelligent life adrift in the soup . . .

2
Dear Frank,
did I ever tell you
about my discovery?

The Milky Way
is a restaurant full of Mexicans.

❋

❋SUPPER LECHE❋

❋

White pillars
white floors
and on a white wall in front of me
the clock has a picture of Sir Walter Raleigh
on it.
          The hour
          is half past his face.

I'm at the counter
perusing a menu
I can't read,
and by the time I put it down
the blind man next to me
has cut his pancakes
into perfect squares.

3
Great men
who
go mad
are always
raving about
their private habits

Nietzsche
writes
an essay
called: "Why I Am So Great"

in which
he tells us
what he had for breakfast!

Well,
today I sauteed onions
in lemon-butter
and simmered
with snails

on my own oven
above 2nd Avenue
the sun at its zenith
drunk as a lord

4
Dear Bob:

re/our phone conversation
of 5–22

Tomorrow I'll be 31
and feel like Ari-of-the-Blessed-Memories . . .

And all I want to know
is what Galileo, down on his knees
before the illusions of another order
muttered under his breath
away from the waxy ears
of the court.

Let me confess,
it seems
we are all alone
in a strange place:

I imagine consciousness
   as a grid
   that changes
   as it moves along a sliding scale,

the face of which
    determines our desires
    and beliefs,

and has a certain resonance
    when stretched
    and held
against the wind, like a perforated membrane.

5
Summer, the inquisitorial length
    of its frustration,
        like Torquemada's nose . . .
Gogol's,
    on his deathbed,
        ablaze with leeches.

In a bookstore
I watch her kneel,
am stunned, like an ambulance
stuck in traffic . . .
           the line of her legs
through diaphanous clothes
             (July had been
a swampy vision,
    but August finds me dumb,
        my own olfactotum a bloodwurst
           after too much sun)
                on route from her toes,
she bends,
        O GOD!

           I go home,
           thumb through *Zen Archery*,
           masturbate and wax invisible.

6
Consider the swimmer
　　　　tangled in eel grass
　　　　　　gathering strength
　　　　to break the surface
　　　　for a breath:
One surge for air,
　　　　　he figures,
　　　and the next to call
　　　for help.
There are divers
　　　　in the distance.
　　　Will they see him
waving from
　　　his net?
　　　　　　　He sits there,
　　　　almost high,
　　having spent
his final breath,
　　　　knees pressed in
　　　　the sand,
a Yogi who accepts,
　　　who views himself
and sees through
　　　his distress
　　　　the current move,
the light develop
　　a clear and timeless
　　　　syntax.

7
A little girl
in a red dress
falls down
in dandelions
laughing at
her own clumsiness . . .

at first
I think her an image
among images, then
see she's the whole poem.

8
I've come back with messages from space, Cynthia.

Mars is barren
but the souls of old reprobates
live in the Crab Nebula
where they generate light at irregular intervals.

We have projected pictures of our nakedness
against the stars
and not one word back about our private parts.

Listening to birds this morning
I'm profoundly sad.
I can hear water in the mountains
rushing underneath the ground, wind in the trees.

It's not a bad feeling, really,
but it seems I've traveled so far to get here.

ADVENTURES IN
IMMEDIATE UNREALITY

MARCEL BLECHER

Translated from the Rumanian by Edouard Roditi

The Rumanian writer Marcel Blecher was born in 1909 in a Moldavian market town where his father owned a tableware store. Blecher began studying medicine in Paris after graduating from a Rumanian high school, but soon had to abandon his studies when he developed tuberculosis of the spine. He then spent the rest of his life, until he died in Rumania in 1938, in various French and Rumanian hospitals. André Breton published some of Blecher's French poems in leading Surrealist periodicals, but Blecher is now considered one of the greatest contemporary Rumanian prose writers. His Rumanian accounts of his illness and his clinical descriptions of his anguished states of mind bear in this respect a curious analogy with some of those of Kafka or of Artaud. Blecher's translator, the American poet Edouard Roditi, has discussed these affinities in an essay, "A Case of Absolute Spleen," published in The Disorderly Poet *(Capra Press Chapbook series, Santa Barbara, California, 1975).*

If I stare for a long while at a single fixed point on the wall, it sometimes happens that I no longer know who I am, nor where I am. Then I become aware of the absence of my own identity, as if I had been transformed briefly into some utterly alien person, and this abstract personality and my own real person struggle on equal terms to dominate my self-awareness.

But my identity returns to me only a moment later, like in those stereoscopic photographs where the two different images remain separate as a consequence of the projector's mismanagement of his equipment, so that they become superimposed only when he gets it all into focus so as to give one suddenly the illusion of relief. Then my room seems to me to have acquired a freshness that it failed to have previously: it returns to its former consistency, and the objects which happen to be there go back to their proper setting, just as a small lump of crushed earth, once dropped into a glass of water, breaks up into layers of different elements, each one of them clearly defined and of a different color. The elements of my room thus settle in the various layers of their own contours and according to the colors of my older memories of them.

The feeling of distance and solitude felt in such moments, when my everyday self has dissolved into inconsistency, is different from any other feeling. If it lasts any length of time, it turns into panic, into the fear that I might never find myself again. Somewhere in the distance, a vague outline of me subsists, surrounded by a broad and luminous aura, like something lost in a fog.

The terrible question then arises: "Who am I really?" It comes to life within me like an utterly alien body that has grown within me, with a skin and organs that are quite unknown to me. To solve this problem, I need a more profound and essential lucidity than that of the mere brain. Everything within my body that can be disturbed now becomes agitated, struggles and revolts in a more elementary and powerful manner than in daily life. Everything within me begs for a reply.

Several times, consecutively, I rediscover my room exactly as I always knew it, as if I were merely closing and reopening my eyes. Each time, my room appears more clearly, like a landscape seen through a telescope as it becomes more and more distinctly focused while we gradually adjust to the right distance and see through the interposed veils of imagery.

Much later, I recognize myself and find myself again in my room with a sense of mild drunkenness. My room is made of a wonderfully concentrated substance. As for me, I am implacably brought back to the surface of things: the deeper the hollow of the wave of uncertainty, the higher too its crest. Never, in any other circumstance, does it seem to me more obvious that each thing must occupy the space that it inhabits, and that I too must be the person that I am.

The torments of my confusion at this point cease to bear a name; all that subsists of it in me is a simple regret that I have failed to find anything in its depths, and the only thing that still surprises me is that so total a lack of meaning should have been able to seem to me to be so closely bound to my most intimate substance. Now that

I have found myself again and am seeking to explain my sensations to myself, I begin to feel that they were of a quite impersonal nature: a simple exaggeration of my identity, which had expanded like a cancer that feeds on its own substance. A tentacle of the jellyfish had stretched out too far and had fumbled in exasperation in the waters before withdrawing beneath its own gelatinous dome. In a few moments of anxiety, I have thus explored all the certainties and uncertainties of my existence, only to return finally and painfully to my own solitude.

After all this, my loneliness is even more pure and pathetic than usual. My sensation of distance from the real world becomes more acute and intimate: a clear and sweet melancholy, like a dream remembered in the middle of the night.

Only this can still remind me to some extent of the mystery and the sad charm of my "fits." Only in this sudden vanishing of my identity can I experience again my former falls into those infernal abysses, and only those moments of lucidity that follow closely my return to the surface can bring before me the whole world, sunken as it was in that unusual atmosphere of uselessness and obsolescence which surrounded me when my trances and hallucinations finally overcame me.

Whether in the streets, at home, or in the garden, the same places always produced my "fits." As soon as I stepped within their limits, I was overcome by the same dizzyness, the same vertigo. Real invisible traps, scattered here and there throughout the city, these places were otherwise quite indistinguishable from other adjoining spots; yet they were there, fiercely lying in wait for me, to make me a victim of the peculiar atmosphere that emanated from them. One step, a single step within these "spaces of damnation," meant immediately a fit, an inevitable fit.

One such space happened to be in the town's public park, in a little clearing at the far end of a path, where nobody ever went for a walk. The wild rosebushes and dwarf acacias that surrounded it left an opening only on one side of it, overlooking the desolation of an abandoned field. Nowhere in the world was there a spot that could seem more mournful and deserted. In the stagnant summer heat, silence settled there in a thick layer that lay on the dusty foliage. Every once in a while, one could hear the sound of some regiment's trumpets, long calls in the desert, distressingly sad . . . In the distance, the air trembled, overheated by the sun, like transparent steam above some boiling liquid.

This spot was both wild and isolated, infinitely lonely. The day's heat seemed to me there to be more exhausting, the air heavier and more difficult to breathe. The dusty bushes were turning yellow in the heat of the sun, as if baked in this atmosphere of desolation, and a weird sensation of sheer uselessness floated in the air above this clearing which existed "somewhere in the world," where even I had come only by chance on a summer afternoon that was likewise devoid of any meaning, an afternoon which had lost itself in the torrid sunshine among some bushes anchored in space, "somewhere in the world." I then felt even more deeply and painfully that I had no business to be in this world, nothing else to do but wander in parks and dusty clearings that were baked by the sun, wild and deserted. This idle wandering, in the long run, broke my heart.

Apart from these "spaces of damnation," the whole town seemed to me to dissolve into a shapeless mass, all equally characterless, with its houses that were interchangeable, its trees that remained exasperatingly motionless, its dogs and vacant lots and dust.

In closed rooms, my fits occurred more easily and frequently. Generally, I couldn't bear to find myself alone in a strange room. If I were obliged to remain alone there, I very soon felt the approach of this sweet but terrible dizzyness. The very room began to prepare itself for it: a warm and welcome intimacy began to be exhaled from its walls and to color surreptitiously the furniture and everything else. Suddenly, the whole room became sublime and I felt happy there. But this was only one of the feints of my fits, one of their perverse tricks, subtle and delicious. After such a brief spell of sheer bliss, everything became confused and topsy-turvy. With eyes wide open, I stared at my surroundings and saw everything lose its usual meaning so as to acquire a new life of its own.

As if someone had stripped them of the tissue paper in which they had been wrapped until now, things suddenly acquired an appearance of ineffable novelty and thus seemed to have been intended for some lofty and fantastic use which could not possibly be guessed.

Things were then seized, moreover, with a real frenzy of freedom and revealed themselves as independent of one another, with an independence which was no mere isolation, but a kind of exalted ecstasy. To me, they communicated their joy of existing in a kind of aura, and I felt they were closely bound to me, clinging to me as I thus became a mere object among other objects, like a vital organ grafted onto live flesh so as to communicate, by means of subtle exchanges, with a body which, until then, had been alien and foreign.

Once, in the course of such a fit, the sun projected onto the wall a kind of small cascade of light, like golden and unreal waters that were laced with luminous waves. At the same time, I could also perceive the corner of a bookcase, with glass doors behind which stood neat rows of leather-bound books, and all these real details of which I was still aware from the very depths of my loss of consciousness completed my sense of being overcome, as if by a final breath of chloroform.

But it was the commonplace and known aspect of things that disturbed me most. The mere habit of seeing them had perhaps finally worn their outer surface threadbare, so that they somtimes seemed now to have been skinned to the quick, as if they were alive, unspeakably live.

In the supreme moment, my fit followed this pattern: I seemed to be floating beyond the frontiers of this world, in a condition that was both pleasurable and painful. If I then heard footsteps approaching, the whole room immediately resumed its former appearance. Within its walls, I perceived an almost imperceptible lowering of its exaltation, and I could conclude from this that the apparent certainties of reality were separated from uncertainties only by a very thin wall.

Again, I found myself in the room that was all too familiar, but now in a cold sweat, exhausted and penetrated by an awareness of the utter uselessness of all that surrounded me. Yet I could also now note new details, which I had never previously noticed, much as one often happens to discover them on something that is otherwise very familiar.

The whole room still retained, however, some memory of the catastrophe, like the smell of sulfur that persists in an area where an explosion has occurred. I could then stare at the leather-bound books, aligned behind the glass doors of the bookcase; in their immobility I seemed to detect a kind of untrustworthy and surreptitious complicity. Objects that surrounded me never abandoned their mysterious attitudes that were fiercely maintained by their truly impassive nature.

In some obscure depths of the soul, words cease to have currency-value. I'm now trying to describe my fits in exact terms, but discover that I express myself only in images. The magic word that might express my fits should derive its power from experienced feelings, and should arise as if distilled from them, like a new perfume produced by a subtle dosing of essences.

It should contain some element of the surprise that seizes me when I watch someone at first in real life and then follow his reflected gestures in a mirror; or it should be like those vertiginous falls that one experiences in dreams while one's very spine tingles with a fright like the lash of a whip, or else like that transparent mist, haunted by bizarre mirages of settings, that one sees drifting in a crystal ball.

After some time, of their own accord my fits ceased to occur, but the memory of them continued to be deeply rooted in me. Adolescence had indeed rid me of my fits, but the crepuscular condition which preceded them and the awareness of the profound uselessness of the whole world which followed them became, so to speak, my habitual state of mind.

Uselessness fills all the hollows of this world like a fluid that would spread everywhere; and the sky above my head, this sky that is always so proper, so absurd and so undefinable, adopted for good the color of despair.

At the very heart of this uselessness that surrounds me and beneath this sky which is damned for all times, that is where I am still aimlessly wandering today.

EIGHTEEN POEMS

CID CORMAN

1

He is a poet:
ergo—one who can
say anything he

likes and get away
with it. Perhaps. But
not unscathed. For he

knowing and obliged
to the death he lives
loves not to escape.

2

Of me—what
do you know?
And do you

really care?
Consider
instead your

own dying.
As it feels
now. Hello.

3 THE SUPERSTITION

Mother—with all that
birdshit over your
stone—you must be far

luckier than you
ever were in life.
But is it your luck

or the birds'? Is it—
in fact—luck at all?
Isn't it all shit?

4

I love you—
yes—you. Of
course—I'm a

nut. Who else
ever loves
any one?

5 THE HOSPITALITY

The mirror's
the home of
the absurd

Take a good
look at where
you are and

realize
you have been
framed. Welcome.

6 THE RIDDLE

There is no
name to this
book—there is

no author
and there are
no words and

not one page
will open.
Yet there's this.

7 WORKING

We look at
each other
from our rooms

and as our
eyes meet—love—
our heart smiles.

8

Speak. Say it.
The word—spit
it out—gra-
tuitous

substantial—
as you can
well hear—as
a bubble.

9

Have you ever felt
like killing yourself?
If so—what stopped you?

Fear? Lack of nerve? Love—
or the hope of it?
Or meaninglessness

in bothering to
assign yourself that
much importance? I

see you are unsure
of any answer
or what you may do.

10

Measure: is:
one's own death.
The breath of

nothing—breathed.
The distance
of a word.

11 THE PROGNOSIS

You are doomed.
Only to
say what you

know. But the
rain falls like
Danaë's

gold and there
are deaths yet
to be born.

12 THE DENOUEMENT

The ghost of Shakespeare
haunting the heights still—
as if he had some

dirty work for us
to do. But we look
beyond the vizor

at the empty face
and recognize him
and know what he wants

is our presence here
in the presence of
his enabling words.

13

Lear—Edward
or King—O
Lycidas!

Out of no
thing nothing—
or all this.

14

And then you are dead.
You. You want to go
out and touch the edge

of the world—simply
to feel and breathe and
be it and be. Like

he day after day
at Mont St-Victoire
becoming Cézanne.

15
Sitting here—
feeling the
words futile—

and silence
futile—and
sitting here

feeling the
words futile—
and silence.

16

So that the
snow comes to
rest upon

snow. As if
no and no
and no came

in the end
to this. This
final yes.

17

New Directions? No
directions. Every
breath spells out the way

the ghost goes. Error
in going—error
in standing still. One

invariably
inches across a
thread over nothing.

18

Night and the
rain fall
together
as if

this had to
be said:
Amen to
amen.

NINE POEMS

RYUICHI TAMURA

Translated from the Japanese by Hiroaki Sato

ETCHING

A landscape he saw in a German etching lies before him. It
looks like a bird's-eye view of an ancient city, dusk turning to
night, or, he thought, like a realistic picture depicting a mod-
ern precipice, midnight being led to daybreak.

The man—that is, he about whom I began to speak—killed
his father when he was young. That same autumn, his mother,
beautifully, went mad.

SUNKEN TEMPLE

People all over the world want proof of death. But no one has
ever witnessed death. In the end, people may be a mere illu-
sion, and reality the greatest common divisor of such things.
Instead of people, objects begin to ask questions. About life.
About its existence. Even if a chair questions, I must be
afraid. Reality may be the least common multiple of such
things. Incidentally, how can a man unable to feel melancholy
about the fate of people stake his life on this world of disturb-

ances? On occasion geniuses have appeared, only to make
nothingness more precise. The self-evident, too, has merely
deepened the turmoil in broad daylight.

Maybe he tried to tell them something. But I'll write only
about facts. First, his knees gave in, hit the ground, and he
fell. Among the people who ran up to him, a young man just
about my age murmured, "A beautiful face. And worse, he
believes in the world like a flower!"

GOLDEN FANTASY

He was afraid of naked thought. Beautiful things never fail to
kill. That's what he used to say.

It's no longer the matter of seeing with the eyes. Nor try-
ing to draw with the hands, either. In broad daylight, in this
city, in the autumn of 1947, I witnessed: the logical proof of
death which someone incises in golden calligraphy on a breast
of white wax.

Nothing is sad, but somehow he stops, eyes filled with tears.
And without saying a word, he is absently looking in my
direction.

AUTUMN

The bandaged rain turned and left. After making a round of
the sleepless city.

That autumn, I went to a recital. A concert hall shut in by
dry doors. A cold, cruel pianist seated on a hard chair. There
the dark dream rejected by sleep silently handed over all
weapons to you. You may arm yourself. Love, love your life.

Outside, the rain smelling of fresh gauze turned another corner to the harbor, from the harbor at twilight to the dark sea, to the world of illusion without stars.

Lips became wet. Soon my hands dried. Goodbye. The woman walked past me and went out. Out the door. A tall man waits for me, getting wet in the rain. To live or to die, with a door between us, we load our guns.

Bless us. Even to us the solitary ones, the enemy has appeared. In the mirror my features totally change. A raw fiction that gives you gooseflesh! Out the door. The sleepless metropolis and its satellite cities. The seven oceans and the enormous desert. From the summer of Petersburg to the winter of Paris. The woman sang ferociously. I still love you, still love you. And Tokyo. Autumn! The world constructed by my hands is dreaming underneath antennas. At this point, ask yourselves about the moment of awakening through the sonata form . . . I pray for the freedom to die. Applause has begun. I stand up from my seat. Mother!

VOICE

The fingers begin to droop. On the gray musical scale unearthed here.

Hold your breath. Talk in voiceless sounds . . . love is a twilight symbol caused by a dissonance of genitals and the dead. On rainy days she is beautiful.

That same autumn, at daybreak, she invites a golden smile. Suddenly I turn my back. The blue that plummets the eye! Death is familiar to me. I witnessed his obscene silence and sacred disintegration. To witness is to experience. I knew the process, first accompanied by screams, then gradually turning to vocatives beginning with *tu*. Sometimes he talked a lot. It was when autumn turned to winter, when fog filled the aquamarine capital. Decline thought. It possesses time. Get out of time. Toward the painful space where you can totally feel. Feel. To feel thoughts with your body. The fingers begin to droop. On the gray musical scale unearthed here. The sounds were selected by my fingers. The sounds were pure matter. A unity was born. Twenty-five years do you have any last words. In the corridor and in the yard, mother is incessantly calling me. It seems it's becoming *tu*. Never pray for the fulfillment of our youth. Weep. If you do, weep like father. If you do, do not weep for father.

PREMONITION

The afternoon arrives suddenly. He, as a person, is pushed into the bottom of the chair. His arms hanging slack, the world begins to darken. The world's sufferings drive him into his single being. The world's sorrows gouge out his eyes. Like an empty socket, the door, opened, leads directly into the past, it seems to him.

From the window the town where he was born is vaguely visible. Rain is falling on the town. For the past twenty years, between the wars, the rain has soaked the ground. The town has changed its shape many times. And the town of his child-hood memory is expunged from this town. Once mother was beautiful, and grandmother must live in the real world as well. The past goes through the door, wordless. And it be-comes connected to a part of the future. The rain collides with time. Before his eyes, the rain is wounded. A bandage! An ordinary middle-aged man walks past holding an ordinary black umbrella.

What can he do? Innumerable hands come through the opened door onto his shoulders, and with a slight pressure cold lips lie on his lips. A kiss without passion. And it's pain-ful, that he tastes deep bliss.

You came to kill me.

THE IMAGE

Beads of death,
in this brown city,
in the rain, throngs of twisted entrails,
black umbrellas, dead experiences, their flow.

The man is not my father, nor is he my solitary friend. I am
merely the same existence, the same experience as he, and a
man with common images. And like him, I was born during
the first world war and surely died in the second.
To fall the way a chair falls! That was my old image, and a
hope for death which the eye in the mud dreamed of.

From the gouged eye, the cracked forehead, the dull gleam
of the hair, and the black clothes wet with sea, the storm, and
the huge illusion, the silent screams, the fierce arias of a ship-
wrecked man, resounding from them, when he appears out of
the weekend night fog that flows when autumn turns to
winter, I have to call out, "Where did you come from?"

My tongue hangs out like a dog's.

THE EMPEROR

There is an eye in the stone. There is an eye closed with
melancholy and tedium.

He passes by my door in a black robe. Winter emperor, my
lonely emperor! With your white forehead reflecting the
shadows of civilizations, you walk to the graveyard of Europe.
The sun shining on your back, your self-punishment is painful.

Flowers! You extend your hands for them. At the end of the
age of reason and progress, the winter of the world is about to
begin. The beautiful European woman is an illusion, and who
will kiss your hand? Is there a budding stage in your palm
which has run dry with brown fate?

Flowers, scars like flowers!

WINTER MUSIC

One can't say it is impossible. At some end of the earth, unknown to me, surely in a basement in a foggy city, a thin twenty-five-year-old just like me, his hair blond, eyes gray, talks in a Scandinavian language about the principle of revolutionary action. Is it madness or sentimentalism? Even if it were vomit in the winter of 1947, who would now believe it was someone else's business? Possibly, like Modigliani's men, he's cocking his head on a thin neck, staring. It's not definite what his eyes are looking at. It's no longer clear. No longer definite. No longer clear, the universe. He is like a man awake in it.

Do not laugh. Even if you met a worm's fate, do not laugh, not now. Whether you refuse it or drag it with you, caress that incomparable, invincible fate.

You, alone, are perhaps the first and last man! I abandon a drama, in a far larger drama.

The singing voice recedes. Arms hanging slack, the noise of innumerable footsteps disappears. From the basement room. From the desert. And the lights of the city turn off and on. Melancholy time forms, solemn rentier's life, farewell!

Even if it is related to a boyhood memory on a summer day or the lonely smell evoked on a snowy night, can you imagine a raw vision unsupported by ideas? But after the pianist, I try to support and to constantly amend a raw vision with my eyes and fingers. The wind begins to blow. Good. The universe gradually turns cold. Eye in the stone! The fingers wish desperately to keep their balance. Should I call an eye larger than my eyes eternity? These moments? The eye has appeared. Hiding a smile, he questions. Regarding the self-evident conquest. An order to massacre! Into the space between the eye and the fingers, into the graveyard of culture, I settle. The winter music.

FIVE HOURS TO VESPERS

MARTIN BAX

A man has placed a hat on the shelving where we want to put our drinks. It is a bowler hat and I can tell, without giving it a friendly rap, that it is one of those hard solid hats—hats which their owners believe impart them some stability, some status in our society. Its owner is red in the face and talking to a lady who is also wearing a hat and all I remember of her face is that it is white—heavily powdered—in contrast to that of her companion. The man glances at us from time to time—wishing, I think, that he was able to persuade his lady to treat him as my lady in treating me.

My lady asked me to take her coat as soon as we had got into the crowded bar and wedged our way across into our corner which is somehow between the food bar and a coatstand now overladen with our coats as well as, no doubt, the coats of the hat owner and the powdered lady. That pair are beyond the coat stand and we find the only place to put our glasses is around on their side of the coatstand just in front of the bowler hat. My lady is not wanting to hold her drink as she wants to slide her hands under my jacket against my shirt while at the same time leaning her whole body against me.

My lady's dress is denim and all down the front there are brown buttons, each rather more than a hand's width apart; I could slip my hand between a pair of them easily. I would love to do that but I have to content myself with saying (which is true) that I would like to undo all the buttons. To which I get the good reply, "I wish you could." And we look at each other eye to eye and we laugh and then Lady, you make another remark, something very personal about my behavior—why you like me—and suddenly my laughter

stops because I can feel tears coming. I lean my head and breathe
deeply saying nothing until I have swallowed. I am suffering/
enjoying all the hysteria that love engenders.

It is an hour we have. I glanced at my watch as we came in. We
would like to be alone in a small room with a bed but we live in a
large city, a conurbation—the urbanation extends not only to the
intricacies of the streets, alleys—through which I walk daily—courts,
yards, precincts, small parks, pools, ornamental ponds, fountains,
palaces all that bit but also to elaborate human structures—wives—
lives intricately connected, work schedules, Marxist memories, ana-
lytical counseling, patterns of people woven so together that when
two move out of their parts they cannot simply align themselves to-
gether, they must creep to another part of the city, find a crowded
hour and stand there at the bar for the time they are allowed. The
time allowed is still (I repeat) only one hour. I glance down at my
watch to detect that most of it has gone.

The thought of the hour we are having, in which both of us have
told the other more of the past, let the other probe into details—"I
swore I'd never tell you that," my Lady said—has entirely eliminated
reservations we had each developed during two days of separation
in our week-old affair and we are both astounded by the way we
feel;—yes this thought, this feel is a good one and thinking this I
remember that quotation about a glorious hour. "One crowded hour
of glorious life is worth an age without a name." When I was fifteen
I used to walk round repeating this hackneyed couplet to myself
and I tell My Lady this. She understands the glory of the hour but
is puzzled by my interest in the quotation: so I glance again at my
watch and read this time the date—March 30th, Monday March
30th.

March 30th, the date is an anniversary of not an ordinary but of
a certain extraordinary Easter Monday. It is the anniversary of the
Sicilian Vespers. The anniversary of that day in twelve hundred and
eighty-two when the Angevins of Sicily were slaughtered by the in-
habitants as the bell rang out for Vespers. These then are the ele-
ments in this story—two lovers, a bar, an hour, a day, and the bloody
end of the Angevin rule in Sicily. What is it that has brought these
elements together (here, now, always)?

In 1282, Charles of Anjou (so Runciman tells us)* was the great-

* The quotations here come from Sir Steven Runciman's brilliant *The
Sicilian Vespers,* published by Cambridge University Press and Penguin.

est ruler in Europe—and wanted to become even greater. The Popes had nominated him King of the Sicilies and with that nomination and his power base in France, he had dominated the Italian peninsula. Now with two rivals—an indolent Southerner, Manfred, and Conradin, a youth from the North of only sixteen who Charles had despicably executed—both rivals then disposed of, Charles stood poised for his greatest adventures. He was aiming for Constantinople; with the blessing of a Pope who had excommunicated an Emperor of the East, Charles's ships, troops, were ready to set out to make him an Emperor of a recombined East and Western Roman Empire.

What my Lady has this to do with you? It is, my love, that you are an Angevin Princess; because you bring with you to me—as did all such brides—wide territories, unrestricted provinces which you lay at my feet. You want to give me you say all your extensive possessions and you flaunt them at me and I take them. I take you for what you are. You are already a Princess of Provence (you told me so yourself) but your dowry includes Toulouse, Carcassonne, Anjou. If our relationship was arranged, was a formal one—which indeed it was—no accident brought us together—yet you yourself are saying to me—"I give it all to you, not only that which I bring in dowry but those deepest parts of myself, my homelands, my own Provence, the seat of my soul which I open to you. Take all I offer you."

From Anjou comes your sternness, because those Angevin ladies (look at the wife of that later King René) they were stern, they could rule. They gave you your tall forehead, your long nose on which one of those medieval helmets could rest. So that René's wife (when he lay in prison) took ship and claimed for him his kingdoms of Naples and Sicily. Anjou gives you that coolness, that assurance I've commented on, that quiet efficiency (I am not well organized) that structuring you wish to give to my life, that ease with which when you tell me of some of your past sadnesses, some of your pains you can say to me (at that point cradling me in your arms) "I can look after Myself."

But your hazel eyes leaning against me here beside the bar belie that confidence. You tell me "I'll open myself to you" and I think then of those areas behind your battlements, behind the fabled towers of Carcassonne, behind the complexities of turret and wall to the intricacies within you. The small square we came across where we sat outside, where the children, of course, ate ice cream, where you calmly concluded several different analyses of my nature.

Taking away from me confused ideas, jumbled computer print-outs, all the mad medley of medieval town planning, you come back with it all sorted out for me, arranged for me to understand like a magic map. Your intellect is busy rearranging my brain.

Which brings me to your hillsides, the orchards of Provence, in winter there are oranges, tangerines and clementines, the fruit trees, the wineyards, the Popperin pears into whose long firm bodies we laid our teeth, those full red grapes we made into wine. (Of the wines of Provence, best known, because it is one of the very few which travels, is Chateauneuf-du-Pape. . . .) The hills and valleys where intimacy takes place, the terraced landscape of your mind where tucked under your hauteur hides (and I saw him by your bed when you invited me there) those poems of the Portuguese Love Songs by the South American genius. You asked me to read one while you cut the cheese and I sipped at that wine. From the seas that border Provence one looks up to great mountains stretching away to columns of snow in the sky—your long white thighs which I tell you about because you seem unaware of them as I compare their beauties to the Alps and then the bower between— the soft garden of ease in your Provence.

Meanwhile another man is disturbing us. I have insisted you eat because you told me that since we met you had lost five pounds— being unable to eat because of me you say. I beg you, my Lady, eat. Quiche Lorraine (of course) and we are nibbling occasionally, you still directing your whole long body against my side and this suited man is suddenly saying, "Excuse me, can I reach round you for the mustard." There on the shelf is a large pot of mustard. We are the sole repositories of mustard in the whole restaurant and, interrupting us again he is back to return the pot and ask me for a knife which somehow again we lock away from him. And I have to detach myself from you and, as he apologizes for disturbing me, I have to say—"Not at all, not at all."

I am back therefore with the time against me telling you about the glorious hour and how I, as a youth, had thought to myself that the glorious hour was what one should aim for. And that I had those sort of ambitions, not exactly the ambitions of Charles of Anjou, not the simple ambitions of megalomania, the urge to rule to have power all that, no there is a difference between me and Charles (surely more than one), but I wanted as a child to achieve something, I knew not what, but I wanted to have honor and glory,

I wanted renown. And I could have all that now, I simply have to state that you are my Queen, that all your wide demesnes have come to me and my fame and glory are assured.

Be wary though that at this moment as I approach my glory, behind me, as behind Charles, lie forgotten enemies. Here is Runciman: is this a description of me? "[They] had drunk well and were carefree and soon they treated the younger women with a familiarity that outraged the [Sicilians]." What followed? "He drew his knife and fell on D. and stabbed him to death. The Frenchmen rushed up to avenge their comrade and suddenly found themselves surrounded by a host of furious Sicilians, all armed with daggers and swords. Not one of the Frenchmen survived. At that moment the bell of the Church of the Holy Spirit and all the churches of the city began to ring for Vespers."

I am sorry that these are unhappy thoughts nor can I fully explain our complex relationship with the Sicilians—perhaps it is this bar. I push you back from me a little and buy you another drink. Shaking my head from side to side I decide I must look away and some of the gray people in the bar begin to acquire faces. I used to come here years ago with Peter and Gavin. It was a quiet place where we would sit upstairs with cheese, a bottle or two of wine and discuss poetry of course and women. Although both can of course do either, Gavin is particularly good on the women, Peter (probably) his peer at poetry.

It comes to me now that in the intervening years this bar has changed, a different breed of men have taken it over. The hat—an absurd relic of an outworn age—is symptomatic of these men of business who have invaded my private bar. Or were they always here and I the invader? I notice now that they are men of conformity, they like an ordered and orderly society. They want people to live in the traditional ways, they are not catholic. If we were very brave you and I might want to burst out of this world but these men have long knives concealed under their coats. But you are tough when I moan and say "This is awful," you reject that, you cheer me. "It is not," you say. You give my love fiber, you encourage me to persist.

The quotation will recur to me later in the day and I suddenly realize that familiar as it is, I do not know its source. Usually it's Shakespeare again when I'm missing a quotation but this time it's someone new who I can't even immediately trace in my companion. The author is Thomas Osbert Mordaunt and there is just the one quotation from him so, apart from the title of his books, all I gain from my search is a couplet which precedes the two famous ones. "Sound, sound the clarion, fill the fife"—well there the sort of martial stuff I expected but then: "Throughout the *sensual* world proclaim, one crowded hour of glorious life is worth an age without a name."

That is something. It is not these men then in this bar who I should be telling about us. It is another world, a sensual world where there are people who will want to know about us. I am telling them now. I have now my lady to help you on with your gray coat which like all your other appurtenances I have learned to love. (I was amazed when you were dismissive of a jacket you wear.) The hour has been extended and we must leave. The choices I sought in childhood are over. They never existed. I shall never live in an age without a name. You and I my lady are fated for some glorious life and there are, yet, five hours to Vespers.

EXALTATION OF LIGHT

HOMERO ARIDJIS

Translated from the Spanish by Eliot Weinberger

> If once a year the house of the dead were to open, and
> the shades shown the great wonders of the world, they
> would admire, most of all, the Sun.—Ficino, *De Sole*

1

Light cast your eyes on our bodies
that our hands moving be weightless
that our deaths not matter
in your land of blue seeds
Cover us light with your glances

2

To we men of the plains
come from far-off times
sailing always
moving always
and though old and sick
always setting out   to travel
give us oh God a place to live
we are tired men

3
Ruysbroeck

in the Green Valley
in the darkness
barely touches
his sacred face

like a light
his hand rises
a sign
illuminates the others

his body is transparent
within
thoughts move
like white flames

around him
the day begins or ends

and joy
like a paradise
the instant diffuses
reaches all

4
a stump   the linden
where as children
we used to speak with God

the walls now peeling
in the room where our parents
once seemed ageless

dry rot has wrecked the wood
of the perpetually blue window

and the bread of the eternal
has been eaten by mold

today the light   always here
opens our eyes

now as then   God
is in the following day

5
these stones
placed on the earth
like eggs in a nest

these trees
near us
flowering

this plain where I am free
where the sun
seems to have stretched out forever

these rays and gusts of wind
following only
their own rhythm

this convergence of beings and things

this present of all
this ruin

6
wounded by time
the poet dies

his heart wakes
in a dream of space

free of the splendors
of the body and its ruins

trembling in light
like the half-gloom of dawn

7

he who is afraid to die feels his time stop
and watching the dawn does not know
if his own sun is setting
then in the festival of light   signs appear
for him alone   bloody
and amid the noise and the voices
he alone hears the distinct and heavy silence
an indescribable maiden makes love to him
her face amid such clarity   full of shadow

8

morning to the beings
that are like a country
seeing them now
is to travel to another place

morning to the eyes
that upon opening have read
the visible poem

morning to the lips
that from the beginning have spoken
the infinite names

morning to the hands
that have touched the things
of the beautiful earth

9

there are beings that are more image than matter
more look than body

so immaterial   we love them
scarcely wanting to touch them with words

from childhood we look for them
more in dreams than in the flesh

and always at the tongue's tip
the morning's light seems to say them

10
To a linden

this hour
wastes
air and men

beneath your shade
I think of beings
and of a country

and I think
if I were a tree
I'd be like you

ineffably I remember
the old tongue that speaks
with beasts and trees

and I feel us unite
in the same consecrated morning

11
birds in the rain are
brief dark flashes
that flock at day's end
to the tree of life

and willow fig or pine
each tree the light reveals
in the damp of the shadows
is the tree of life

12
here I am well
in the time of my spirit

facing this mountain
a high thought
that like a womb of light
has crystallized

seeing this poem progress in its words
and love born
like the spiritual fruit of the day of all

turning on my own pivot

while the lioness creates her lions
the fig tree its fruit

13
come ancestral poet   sit
take the shadows from your mouth
shake the darkness from your clothes

come to this morning
that seems to last forever
and just appearing
seems ancient
and eternal

come to this mountain
that raises its white peaks
like pure thoughts

to this river
that flows from darkness
into night
crossing the day
like a white god

come to this moment
and give these things that are leaving
a verse now

14
I'm traveling
sitting, walking, I'm traveling motionless

through the house, through the hour, through the river
I'm traveling through the body that travels

through mountains and looks and beds
to the sun   to the air

through mysterious clay to the infinite

I never stop traveling

15
this flame
rising neither hot nor cold
delivers from its crown to the earth
a benediction of rays

perhaps it is a song
or a visible letter
this tree
with its many slopes
to the sky

spirit of the forest
lord among flowers
this child of earth and water
is the visible air

with branches pointing to the ground
it rises to the sacred

this light
this tree

16
I walk among words toward silence

writing until the ink stops

now that I know
that my song will stop
at night   with my body

17
Lago dell'Averno

ripples move with the wind-gusts
frogs talking in the mud
red fish in the air are
an arc that tenses
and light piercing the shadowy nests
criss-crosses like a tangled mane
a backwater is a flower
open to the water's depths

behind every eye the human eye watches
the color of beings is living flesh
the lake is a quiet look
only night enters in

18
for pure clarity the water speaks

time runs above the quiet light

towers white   the city is weightless

the mountain peaks far off
touch eternity   touch time

NATURAL FRONTIER

NÉLIDA PIÑON

Translated from the Brazilian Portuguese by Giovanni Pontiero

TRANSLATOR'S NOTE. *Nélida Piñon is generally regarded by critics to be one of the most interesting young writers to have emerged in Brazil during the early 60s. Her first novel,* Guia-Mapa de Gabriel Arcanjo *("Guide-Map of the Archangel Gabriel"), was published in 1961, and there has been subsequently a steady output of fiction, notably two prize-winning novels,* A Casa da Paixão *("The House of Passion," 1972) and* Tebas do Meu Coração *("My Beloved Thebes," 1974), and a remarkable collection of short stories titled* Sala de Armas *("Fencing Room," 1973), from which the text translated here has been extracted.*

The bold, experimental nature of her prose, with its sustained ambiguity and dense metaphors and symbols, conveys the unmistakable impression of a trenchant and powerful sensibility. Her wholly personal style expands into complex meditations enhanced by multifaceted images and a tense lyrical phrasing which betray the influence of surrealism and existentialist phenomenology.

In a lecture addressed to a literary congress held in Rio de Janeiro in July 1976, the author provided some valuable insights into her own individual approach. "As a writer," she said, "I work with that most intangible of all materials—creation—as fine as the texture of a spider's web yet capable of reproducing itself purely from saliva, thus forsaking all ballast and brilliance. . . . Perhaps no other narrative of mine better illustrates my private poetics and daily attitude to my role as a writer than 'Natural Frontier,' with its subtle exploration of frontiers and the ultimate lines of demarcation. . . ."

He left for hell on the stroke of twelve noon. By a familiar road which all the village knew. It had always been thought of as the natural frontier. There was no guard there to prevent the wayward. On the contrary, the perfume which came from within was soothing. Those who finally decided to visit the place claimed that they suddenly felt attracted or were simply curious to investigate. Although many of them gave up the idea amidst convulsions and escapes.

In discussing this journey, which became the favorite topic of conversation in those parts, people advised discretion. Those who intended to go beyond hell's boundaries, perhaps yielding to some inner impulse to pursue other destinations, were fully aware of what awaited them.

Most of them stayed there forever, absorbed perhaps by death, for there everything spoke of death. And what other reason for existence could that strange realm possess, when they doubted that one might find there even one enraptured soul.

Those, however, who did succeed in returning went on living under a cloud of suspicion, strangers now in the land where they had learned the art of fencing, and the passionate pursuit of the sun.

They went around tearing off their clothes until they were stark naked, searching for some return to a more primitive nature after that experience of intense intimacy. But no physical disorder could restore to these former inmates of hell the experience which they had known. As if the form of man had been so perfected in its last stages of evolution that not even hell could change the design traced out millennia before. The idea, therefore, that hell wished to create its own race was denied with the return of some of the adventurers.

Those bodies without trace of punishment aroused in those who questioned them the suspicion that they, who had not visited hell, were also assisting in the absurd. They then began to look for some resulting deformities, for the expression of those creatures did not correspond to what one expected of a human being. The task they set themselves was both arduous and unrewarding. Particularly as these former inmates uttered sounds of some remote, primitive tongue, presumably the outline of a language still seeking its form. And there was nothing to suggest that they had all been to the same gardens or inhaled the perfume of the same flowers. For each expressed himself with a different sound which was never adopted by all of them, although the inhabitants of the village knew little or nothing about language. They presumed, nevertheless, to voice opinions about everything, and one day they might geld animals by scientific methods or change the course of certain rivers.

In addition to this strange language with its alien sounds, each so individual and so rigorously limited, their eyes became fixed on obscure points whose direction one could never hope to trace. Nor did they recognize companions who, unlike them, had remained on earth. The inhabitants of the village came to the conclusion that they had taken leave of their senses. At any rate, their judgment of things differed completely from that which they had expressed before leaving. Now they were plunged into oblivion and none of their gestures suggested in any way the existence which they had previously known on earth. They no longer remembered their own community and felt only nostalgic for a world that must have been richer.

The youth, however, expressed his desire to depart when he reached the age of twenty. He was handsome and admirably pure. The most well-loved young man in the village. His body suggested the smoothness of spotless linen and the discipline of temple choirs. He asked forgiveness of his enemies and the patience of his many friends and companions. And just as he had always cultivated an austere way of living, he now devoted himself to his last farewells. The adventure itself surpassed his heroic powers. Instead of exploring new territories, he was seeking awareness inside a chrysalis, the first of many complications. Hell had suddenly become his most intense link with earth. Yet it remained the most remote path of all. His chosen vocation.

His mother rent her garments, and wept inconsolably on the eve of his departure. Without saying a word, his father took him by the arm and made him walk the streets of the village under the harsh glare of the sun. Each road was lined with its madmen. For no household failed to put its treasure on show. They exhibited the former inmates on the verandas specially built to receive them, where they remained until dusk. When they gathered indoors, they momentarily succeeded in banishing those obstinate expressions on the inmates' faces and those curious sounds one might easily associate with a dead language. The youth allowed himself to be led. He gazed upon everything as if for the last time. Another way of seeing things was yet to steal over him and he yearned for the moment of change. Gracing the verandas, these creatures waved their arms as if clutching the claws of writhing spiders, or even tiny winged insects, while drawing them close to their skin. A strange atmosphere shrouded the landscape. Bright yet hazy. An intensity which the village willed itself to accept. They could not kill the former inmates for everyone feared that race dedicated to divinity. The youth began to understand his father's warning. He considered the procession both solemn and regal if only the village itself were not so humble.

When the day arrived, he was careful to carry bread and a flask of wine. These were his last whims. The church clock was striking twelve and no other sign guided him. Beyond communication, the youth simply knew. He looked at the elders of the village, perhaps assuring them of an unprecedented return, should they but confide in his gospel. Although he might start to speak with the strange agglomeration of sounds which the former inmates used as proof of the rich linguistic resources of hell, his language would have to revert to country speech when talking to the inhabitants of the village. He must remain quietly obedient to the laws of tradition.

While some of the villagers could understand his haste, the village as a whole completely deplored the mental collapse of this twenty-year-old youth. A sacrifice made under the pretext of lucidity. The villagers, silencing their fears, accompanied the youth hoping that he might abandon his decision. They lost sight of him as he approached the frontier and when he reached the gates of hell, he did not linger. Brave and solitary he entered those gates as if he were mounting a splendid thoroughbred horse, a performance worthy of the hour.

After his departure, people could speak of nothing else. It was always the same. Each man lost to the community was eagerly discussed. More than the loss itself, the villagers were bothered by the reasons which led them to this mysterious destiny. What attracted them above all was their ignorance of the world—a disquieting possession.

On days such as these, the villagers stopped working and started to live on reserve supplies from the abundant harvests of earlier years. They were continually to be seen consulting the hour, for their notion of time was of an acid precision. And they persisted in the worship of their ancient gods. And hell, uncomfortably close, watched over them. These villagers had all descended from a race which traditionally cultivated stones and leaves. The stones resisted any restoration either by hand or tool. However irregular, their original form was preserved. The leaves were chosen from trees known to have survived for a hundred years.

There was always a limit to the stay of those who finally returned, and once that limit had expired, the pilgrim knew himself to be lost. Even while ignoring to what extent the journey through that hemisphere relied upon vague perception or an express prohibition. The reason for this persistent interest in the former inmates, whose existence was so rare that its anguish was engraved upon their faces, was so that they might teach others the rules of the nearby territory. It was sufficient to approach that frontier in order to feel an unmistakable sensation of burning.

The villagers, however, wavered when confronted with those strange sounds. In all probability this strange language concealed interesting ideas perhaps even advanced to the point of surpassing the material needs of any given moment, and equipped with a system of reasoning which the village would only be able to grasp after millennia. And the half-witted expressions on the former inmates' faces concealed these powerful discoveries. Only their mobile fingers responding to some strict but undefined code with its own peculiar script testified to human origins, and to links with a race which not even the journey through hell had succeeded in destroying.

The villagers were convinced that the brilliant ingenuity of this twenty-year-old youth must be waning daily. From a distance, they accompanied his movements, his body perhaps already undergoing laceration of the flesh, his innocent face on the point of deciphering cruel truths. For he had entered therein as a monarch professing his own laws. But with the passing of the years they began to realize that they had lost him forever.

His mother went into mourning. She did not even have the consolation any longer (a consolation which it had taken her ages to accept) of leading him out every afternoon on to the veranda which they had just finished erecting. She felt that her son's journey was destined to exhaust all resources.

Even if they did not recognize officially that form of death, the villagers understood that the uneasy truce between hell and earth maintained by the sacrifice of their best men had now entered upon a belligerent phase. Previously the community had amused itself in badly designed little skiffs when they braved the seas. And as if that were not enough, they had accumulated the experience of several battles. No emotion was neglected. They behaved like mortals.

Now, stalked by temptation and driven by a reckless spirit of adventure, they began to experience fear. As if the tentacles of some animal of an unknown species were fastened round their necks, choking them to death, or a plume of smoke had entered their lungs already flooded with water. In time, fear had become the most obvious sense of being alive. Then they would recall those happy days when hell was remote and people did not set off to look for it. Its present nearness injured them. It beckoned them with urgency. They prayed at such moments with pleas addressed to hell rather than to their gods of stone and leaf. It became impossible to bear that truth situated at the bottom of the pass of that greater summit.

Until one bright dawn, the youth left hell by the door through which he had entered. Looking resplendent, even gallant, and certainly more handsome. Prepared for a love which would suffocate him in some other way. He greeted no one during the journey, although the news of his return soon spread and everyone came to gaze at him. He seemed to possess some strange power which prevented him from colliding with objects in this world, without actually seeing them. He spared flowers and insects of unusual splendor as if he had eyes in his feet and shared the timeless ease of birds in flight. Nevertheless, he did not grow wings. His long stay in hell did not impose this obligation. The only certainty he brought back was confined to a pattern of life that was almost religious.

Faced with this new alliance between the sovereign lands, the people responded with shouts and cries. An atmosphere of mourning outweighed that of rejoicing. For the youth's return did not rule out the possibility that he too, like the others, might have been doomed. He adopted that strange tongue which would deprive him of their society. But they were prepared to forgive him his frontier speech, overwhelmed as they were by the sheer joy of regaining a lost soul. Hope now began to encourage them into new ways of behaving.

The boy's parents and brothers and sisters wept with joy. Here at last, the son and brother they had believed lost in the shadows of hell was restored to them. Returned from that hell to which he had departed years before on the stroke of twelve noon, when he announced his glorious innocence to all. Yet it was still uncertain whether his eternal pact with hell might not deprive him of his basic virtues by altering some vital organ of his body. He was behaving exactly like those villagers who had never left earth. All of them belonging to the same tribe, and ready to consider him the pride of their race, which devoted itself to hunting because of their noble origins.

And when the youth returned without offering any explanation to the community, they without even criticizing his slowness of mind, which after all had been exposed to the sun, acclaimed him as if he had come bearing gold and silver. In truth, there was no corruption in his body. Some observed in his expression a certain disdain for the landscape, he who had abandoned the region of dazzling light. And his gestures betrayed the disquiet of someone adapting himself to the laws of vegetation. His light footsteps, his delicate manner of treading paths without so much as grazing them. No longer dependent upon the solidity of objects in order to be received once more among men. As he contemplated plants and birds, he appeared to consecrate them, as if caught up in some mysterious ritual of disharmony. His hands held aloft, reached out to everything around him and his controlled movements suddenly infused them with new life. As if hell had taught him how to recover limbs damaged forever or faculties destroyed by some movement of human terror.

The novelties which the youth brought with him began to alarm the villagers. That curious manner of staring into space, his preoccupation with cleanliness before a nature with which all identified themselves or refused to see reformed. That youth would never submit himself to the ritual of the veranda specially erected for his return. His happiness was to awaken that light of rare intensity, rejoicing in the creation of a world which his devotion brought into existence. Animals became tame at his side and abandoning the forest, the ravens in amorous exaltation followed him. He had attained the self-reliance of someone who had lived in excess with the miraculous and beyond its malignity he must accept nothing more.

He ignored his father, his mother, and the company of mortals. Lord of the plough and the seeds, he went on consuming his daily share of miracles. Astonishment swept the village. The villagers followed his footsteps and did not abandon him even for an instant. The objects which he distractedly overturned after having consecrated them were carried into the houses. Placed beside the bread on tables, the villagers examined these objects trying to detect the forgery.

Among themselves they questioned whether they, too, might be

capable of restoring nature and the seminal world, once they peace-
fully came to settle there and participated in its destiny. Or whether
there also might exist some clandestine nature from which they
were excluded because of their inherent condition as earth-bound
mortals. Yet they wondered why the earth, if not created for ordi-
nary mortals, should allow such monsters to settle there. And since
they were incapable of enjoying earth by the only means of com-
munication at their disposal, what other forms of life should they
struggle to possess which would finally permit them to incorporate
themselves with the vision from which they had been hitherto
excluded.

Their uncertainties hovered between honey and fruits. While
they could demand from the youth some form of speech, unlike the
other former inmates, he lived in silence. He despised signs, sound,
and their alien language. His behavior only served to intensify the
villagers' fears and the entire village began to question its own fate.
They were well aware that the youth was utterly remote from earth,
yet they could not but follow his example. They found themselves
transformed into an entanglement of entrails, obliged to a sex which
they chose to practice in hours of bitterness, always to end up in
tears. Not even the most detached part of their body saved them.
And among themselves, they were unable to communicate. To in-
dulge in hatred was much more easy, that sentiment ever masked
among painful alliances.

It was raining when the villagers finally assembled in the town's
only square. No one spoke in defense of an earth already written
off as lost. They must abandon their homes, their venerable dead,
and their abundant stores. They did not even take their leave of the
former inmates. They carried only their blood, which became agi-
tated to the point of demanding reality.

The villagers set off in procession. The entire village. They knew
the route and trod its pavingstones with respect. Along that road
more honorable companions had preceded them. They only halted
when they came to the entrance of hell, whose solemnity impressed
them, although its great gates were closed to them. Like bulls in a
fury of strength they repeatedly charged those gates in the hope of
knocking them down. But they failed even to shake them.

There was no one there to explain why they must abandon the
idea of hell, now that the whole race had decided to take up resi-
dence there forever. All they could discover was a tiny inscription

over the entrance whose words they read attentively. There was no final destination to be reached after all. The inscription simply said that hell had been removed to another place and no details were given.

THE OTHER SLEEP

H. C. TEN BERGE

Translated from the Dutch by Peter Nijmeijer

Gray light, late swans in straight flight
    past slight outlines of receding mountains

having traveled by celestial horse from fergana
    and now at the edge of stiffened morasses

south of the road that branches out on the autumnal plateau:
    a notion of vapor around mounted nomads,

flash of a train red-dusty breaking from the mountain flanks—
    and low in the western basin the crème yolk of the sun.

led by guides, ill-practiced but well
    equipped I sit here on moss among meager birches

poking the ashes of a time-worn fireplace;
    damp nostrils, eyebrows bristly with frost

too late an early white-hare gets wind
    of the preying fox

Numbered here among the mopers,
    there excluded as a sorehead

I claim to know of nothing else
           than what's developed or develops by my hand;

remained ignorant through thinking,
           in everything the beginner who unlearns

and then attempts again
           to lay a fire with damp wood.

cracking, moaning, nonetheless
           delving in dreams for ancestral forms:

the hare grilled finally! but then, with a crick,
           to be carried tentward bent as a try square

by curious hunters (who had heard
           that the tsar would be killed long ago)

That shows great promise when the revolution
           of the estranged will soon uproot the city!

although recovered the body falters yet
           in immense emptiness

and the mind is felled by obscene silence
           like a birch tree;

oh cool womblike
           earth, even the pliable spear of the slow and

distant sun chafes your skin here like a shingle
           skimming over water,

the cold of ages keeps
           the earth's crust benumbed, summer and winter—

only the expired penetrate her;
           the rustling of rats swells in the shrubs

Troubled lies, in his tent on the terp
         the stubborn sucker from the west

who only sleeps to seize
         the sleep eventually,

who thinking of sunken lives
         slowly sinks himself into the dark tidal forest below.

the sopping lowlands stiffen,
         the growing frost discloses the morass;

fur hunters rifle him awake: dragged along
         into which present? hitting upon prehistoric loot

in the bog? (dead mammoths still bear living
         germs of anthrax under their skin;

gray as bats and stale as sheep the flesh beats
         the eager eaters with eternal sleep)

Remember images of people,
         tough and supple as a backbone:

the girl of Windeby—she with the blindfold,
         strangled in the peatbog and tanned

like cowhide among oakbark;
         the reddish venus of Yde, her corpse

full of grease, the Grauballe man—caught
         in fright, with violated throat,

disposed of life
         like a text of its meaning,

but still pinned down by bifurcated stakes
         to the bottom of the peatbog

and then covered with willow branches,
        tough and supple as a backbone

"in the moss-grown basin at the tree line"

A grave; the tardy digging begins,
        layer after layer slowly spaded away:

a soapstone bowl and traces of fire,
        we hit upon signs—

clotted language
        scratched into an oracular tooth.

then, through the fracturing lines in the stony mud
        breaks the veiled double image of black eyes

—as from dead lovers, surprised in the act
        of coition and never recovered by friends;

racked by time and accident
        but now a prey to frozen ecstasy—

still expecting birth
        and busy yet with death

Is the raven flying yet?
        is the bear loose again?

here, under the wide-rimmed hat
        of cattlemen and vicars,

tight in the saddle—the horsefly
        crushed against the forehead,

along the road that branches out,
           between receding pinewoods and approaching plateau—

where the woods thin out like poet's hair,
           on the border of hoofbeat and heaven's lightning

we say goodbye
           and extinguish the sparks

and the slumber is roused to feed
           the senses with signs of emptiness and life

1977 REFLECTIONS

CARL SOLOMON

My Changing View of France

My earliest picture of France and of Frenchmen was one of men with finely waxed thin mustaches and round hats with visors who spoke through their noses and were always saying things like "Vive La Fwance!" They also said things like "Ils ne passeront pas," guarded the Maginot Line, detested the Boche, and always sang songs like "La Marseillaise'" and "Frère Jacques." They always seemed slightly effete but were very gallant.

For a long period, this image of France disappeared and was replaced by that of Resistance fighters wearing raincoats and furtively sneaking up and down alleyways. This soon blended into the picture of the French existential tough, cigarette sticking miraculously to his lips in all hectic situations, who shrugged, always shrugged, when anything tragic, hair-raising, or heart-rending occurred.

This touched off a period of expatriatism in me when I actually went to France and picked up a million and one intimate details of actual French life to fill out the picture. My accent changed, I knew some current argot, popular songs, current poets and painters, the names of existent streets and cafés. This became somewhat watered down and became a peculiar blend of French and Jewish mannerisms when my expatriatism became limited to the Fifties Greenwich Village scene. From expatriate to Francophile during that also brief period.

Eventually, though, Greenwich Village became cut off to me also, and my scene changed into the original American Jewish scene now free of the fifties-ish existentialist elixir. The Jewish Shrug replaced the French Shrug. And, lo and behold, I began to think of Frenchmen as wearing thin mustaches again and always coming out with "Vive La Fwance!" I stopped reading Prévert, Quenueau, Michaux, and *Les Temps Modernes* and settled for what I could get in my neighborhood public library. I began reading Victor Hugo, Dumas, Balzac, P. C. Wren's *Beau Geste*, etc. Again, as in childhood, I began thinking of French as "a beautiful language." Adieu Rimbaud, Céline, Genet, Baudelaire, de Sade and ship ahoy our NATO allies. I maintain that this is now the only viable view of France for me. A Frog is a Frog is a Frog. Any other attitude would, in the resurrected native philistinism, mark me as a "weirdo."

Apropos the Taj Mahal

Nobody at all mentions the Taj Mahal these days. Yet it was one of the great romantic dreams of my childhood to see the Taj Mahal. Some iconoclast might even shatter convention by jumping into and swimming around in its pool. Richard Halliburton in, I believe, *The Royal Road to Romance* (or was it *The Flying Carpet?*) had a shimmering photograph of the glistening dome in one of the high points of his very popular travel and adventure book. My father, an avid reader, often mentioned this fabulous tomb built by a great emperor for his deceased wife. And it was a dream of my childhood someday to see the Taj Mahal. But the romantic dreams of one decade are, alas, not the romantic dreams of a decade forty years removed. My poet-friend Allen went to India in the early sixties, and I even drank champagne with him, Peter Orlovsky, Louis Ginsberg, LeRoi Jones (Imamu Baraka), and some other people in his cabin on the *America* just before sailing time. And Allen never once (as I recall) mentioned the Taj Mahal in his writing about India. One of my female cousins married a young Pakistani in the seventies and took a trip (well, to Pakistan not India) with him and was never under the spell I am probably still under—the idea of the Taj Mahal as being one of the wonders of earth. For that matter who ever speaks these days of the wonders of the earth? Maybe Allen Ginsberg himself is one of the present-day wonders of the earth. During World War Two, many Americans served in the China-India-Burma theater, and I suppose many of them may have been under the old spell and did visit the glistening dome, etc. They were probably the last. When I was a seaman some ships I might have caught went to Karachi and might have set in motion such an adventure for me, but other forces were in motion in my mind just then and the lure of the Occidental *caveaux* of St. Germain des Prés held a greater attraction for me. Sensibility had even by then so changed.

It is very likely technology which brings about these decade by decade changes in one's fantasy-life. There was a day when Lautréamont could get a rise out of me with Maldoror's sexual adventures with female sharks. This seemed superreal at that time. Yet fairly recently I glimmed some flicks showing women making it with horses and pigs and dogs, and at that moment Lautréamont seemed, fateful word, to have been *absorbed*. As Artaud has been absorbed and the Taj Mahal has long ago been absorbed.

Searching for a new *frisson* to keep my mind from withering away and to keep the old excitement still alive, I try desperately to hitch myself to this magical technology which plays so alchemically with men's minds. I learned to operate a computerized cash register and experienced something of a Marinetti-like thrill at this futurism-of-the-seventies. I, simple me, touch the button, and it connects with an enormous Rube Goldberg machine somewhere computing enormous records. Marinetti was the poet of fast cars *circa* 1920 and was the prophet of Neal Cassady and of Marlon Brando's popularity. He eventually was killed fighting against the Soviet Union on the Eastern front in World War Two. There was a conflict even then among those seminal poets and thinkers of the early century centering around technology, the then new technology. Some, like Marinetti, felt that the speed, the *élan*, was the revolutionary thing, the motif of change. Others, socialists of that day, felt that the social and economic changes brought about by the technology would touch off the really important revolution. Cocteau's famous Nazi-like motorcyclists with their homosexual etcetera on the one hand and treatises on what the production of motorcycles etcetera would do to the relations between capital and labor (this as the Hegelian-Marxian crux) on the other hand.

I feel this conflict of ideas about motivation for the new technology as I press, button by button, the keys of my magical computer register. My labor, the cost of my labor, the final product, surplus value milked from my labor, etcetera, etcetera.

Marinetti died on the Russian front, on that cold damned Russian front. And we all know what Marinetti finally stood for. Where were his fast cars then? Where were Cocteau's Nazi-like motor-cyclists? And Rommel's dashing turned-up hat?

Which should bring us back to talk, nostalgic, etcetera from a balding man about childish dreams, encouraged by his father, about the Taj Mahal—still a glistening monument to an emperor's deceased wife—but now ignored by glamorizers everywhere.

THE HONEY TREE SONG OF RASEH

Translated from the Bidayuh Dayaks of Sarawak, East Malaysia, Borneo, by Carol Rubenstein

Introduced by Jerome Rothenberg

INTRODUCTORY NOTE

Jerome Rothenberg

In the month of July, 1970, the poet Carol Rubenstein left New York City & started on a literal "adventure in poetry" that few poets before her had attempted. It brought her after many travels to the aboriginal peoples of Borneo, who were the keepers of an ongoing oral tradition: a contact with the powers of *poesis* that was integral until recently to their culture, peripheral or despised in our own. The point has been made many times before, & I don't want to belabor it here. We aren't bereft of poetry either, but few of "us" still have it at the center of our lives, & having given that central place to other goods/other gods, we live estranged from the imagination—a course that we prepare for "them" in turn.

So the revelation comes to her in the three years spent gathering a massive number of songs & narratives & incantations: that the mind—poetic mind itself—is still alive there. "The Honey Tree Song of Raseh" here published is a single example from the 1400 page book she ends up with, but it's typical enough of the riches at hand —the oral poet's openness to what exists around him. From the vantage of the singer—the young man climbing up the tree in search of honey—the life of the village & what surrounds it opens out. "This place" becomes "the world." Clusters of images & events intersect in & with the singer's thoughts & actions: the tree, the bees, the people bathing, fishing, as he builds the ladder, climbs it; distant images of dying children, strangers on their way to visit, animals & birds; the wind, the image of a young girl conjured up he draws there with the same torch that drives the bees out; the sounds of children in the morning, lovers walking crabwise in the water, bees returning to their hive. And still the meanings come, because the song, she says, "is actually a prayer, magic-making, invoking & blessing all that is involved in collecting honey, & all the sweetness of life. . . ."

This "progress of the images that make up the poems & provide their natural structuring" is, as Rubenstein herself writes, "not different in essence from poems anywhere." But most closely it resembles—in its quick movements, its creation of a diverse field of multiple occurrences, its shifts of order from performance to performance—the frontiers of our own poetic experiments in the century now drawing to a close. So it becomes possible to see, even to imagine that one hears that sound (at least the movement of that deeper mind) that leads the singer-poet through his world. It is a great human work: endangered in its habitat, drowned out by sounds our own world brings there. Something of this she helps us salvage—for the species' good.

TRANSLATOR'S NOTE.

A "honey tree," a tree that attracts bees so that beehives are found on it, is selected, and on it a rough ladder is made. A young man carrying a torch climbs up and climbs along the branches, which is without hand rails and often quite high up, in order to smoke the bees out of their hives and to collect the honey. Climbing the honey tree, eating the honey, and singing these songs are times of much festivity for the village. The song is actually a prayer, magic-making, invoking, and blessing all that is involved in collecting the honey, and all the sweetness of life, and has very ancient roots.

The rhinoceros beetle—the heavy gurgling sound.
The cricket—the high insisting sound.

The rhinoceros beetle says this comes first,
the cricket says that should be first—
the words of the honey tree song.
The seeds that come from the land near the sea
are big as that in the beak of the little kunchih bird.
The flowers of the honey tree
are big as that in the beak of the ordinary bird from Java.
The chips fallen while making the rungs
of the ladder to go up the honey tree
are big as that in the beak of the hornbill.
Honey tree found by my grandfather when he was lost in the jungle,
found by my grandmother while she was hunting with a blowpipe,
found by my father while he was out walking.
Planted by a tiny short-quilled porcupine and his wife,
planted by a big long-quilled porcupine and his wife,
planted by a pheasant on the edge of the jungle,
planted by a moonrat on the edge of a hill,
planted on the edge of the junction of two rivers,
planted between two ponds.

How big is this *tapang* tree which has just been planted?
It is as big as the hairpin of a girl called Dayang Dia,
the hand span of the padi leaf,
the finger span of the bamboo leaf—
a hand span when it first appears,
a finger span as it starts to grow.
The form of the tree, its wideness, this growing *tapang* tree,
found by my grandmother while fishing with a poison root.
To make a single step for the tree, I work the whole day.
Every year I make another ladder—
a single step, a whole month.
I make the steps to become my footpath;
my ladder will turn into the vining root of the *kayu ara* tree.
To cast a spell on the bamboo spike to turn it into silver,
to cast a spell on the bamboo rail to turn it into lead,
to cast a spell on the *tibadu* vine that it become colored thread,
for the knot which I tie to grip like the claws of the owl.

Knock knock—
I hammer at the nest of the myna bird in a hollow of the tree.
Knock knock—

the Malays are making the sides of their big boat.
Very sharp, my stakes of *buluh dindang* bamboo,
very sharp, my iron chisel for fighting against the *tapang* tree.
The feet of the mousedeer stumble as he staggers
carrying a piece of bamboo for the floor.
Knock knock—
the young bachelors are hammering at the *tapang* tree.
The *tapuh* tree grows crookedly,
pointing to a girl in the lower part of Kuran river;
my body bends crookedly while I make the rungs
of the ladder to go up the honey tree.
The *tapuh* tree grows crookedly, pointing to a girl at Kuran;
my body bends crookedly while I make the steps
which become the vining root of the *kayu ara* tree.

How long will the young men bathe,
bathe in the river near the foot of the *sibau* fruit tree?
How long will it take for the young men to climb,
to climb the single *tapang* tree?
Let me pass behind you, grandmother of my friend.
I want to go up to visit my youngest sister, Limpunai Bunchu,
who is suspended high in a high cloud.
How long will the young men bathe,
bathe in the river near the foot of the *sibau* fruit tree?
How long will it take for the young men to climb,
to climb the single *tapang* tree?

The *jawah* seeds which are falling in clusters
are eaten by a big *samaring gading* cock
while he is watching a girl who happens to pass by.
My feet ache from twisting at the tree,
my hands ache from gripping the tree.
A small child from Sinangkan village is dying of hunger
because he has eaten the blood of the big ground worm.
I hammer at the first branch,
making the other branches nearer and nearer
which all look like the inner ribs of a big boat.
My very sharp chisel, called Belantikai,
was bought by my mother and father from Brunei traders.
My very sharp chisel with its round edge
fights against the tree knob, which is twice a tree.

I hammer to make it go in deeper and deeper,
to stick in place until the knife's sealing gum drips out.
The gold-colored *gading* coconut is my sitting stool
and is my chopper of fish bones.
There are many knobs on branches to rest upon each trip.

Sleep, my little dog, sleep.
Your sleep is disturbed but by mosquitoes come from the swamp.
Sleep well and continue guarding
the store of padi and the store of money.
To carry water and to keep good reserves of water.
To pound padi and to keep good reserves of rice
to entertain the strangers who will soon be coming,
the greedy stranger with the pot belly,
the young stranger with a bad smell of urine.
Draw no water at *tangit* pool, it is infested with crocodiles.
Draw water, you young girls,
at a rocky corner in the shallows of a stream.
Do not rip the torn shirt further while washing it in the stream,
lathering it with the foaming skin of the *langir* fruit.
The girl who always wanders and visits is warned by her lover.
The *tak-terang* bird is pecking
on an old *meruat* tree at the back of the padi store.
Do not stay up late at night, you young girls,
or in the morning you will rise too late.
The *siluang* fish, poisoned by the *tuba* root,
can be seen dying at the edge of the pool.
Which of you young men has a heart so brave and daring
he will walk unaided the length
of the branch of the *kayu ara* tree?

Tonight I call the wind,
the wind called up from the foot of the *tuba* tree.
I am not calling the wind belonging to other people,
I am calling the wind from the village.
I call the wind from Buguh where the people know everything.
Why is the wind delayed in coming here?
I am calling the wind of the very clever people of Enchangi.
Why is the wind delayed in its shaking of coming and going?
Rough wind, harsh wind lives on the top of the honey tree.
Smooth wind, light wind, stay, delay your going away.

Tonight I call the wind,
the wind called up from the foot of the *tuba* tree.
I am not calling the wind belonging to other people;
I am calling the wind of my sweetheart,
someone who is well known to everyone.

Why has her wind not come?
She is taking leave of the child, who falls and stumbles after her.
The pig's tail is waving;
it has stolen the smoked foods on the drying platform.
My tail is waving to visit you, young girl, breast-feeding.
The rat's tail is waving;
it has stolen the smoked foods on the drying platform.
My tail is waving, leaning over and trying to see my sweetheart
who sits at the farthest end of the longhouse.
The branch of the *tuang* tree is dry
which I dried on top of the fireplace.
Between my thighs I squeeze the soft breast of the young girl.
Asking for fish paste, bought for cooking the *sibemban* fish;
asking for the favorable south wind to blow.

I shine the flare of the torch on the bees,
and the bees move to another knob of the branch.
I shine the flare of the torch again—the bees go farther.
Go down, you bees, go down;
follow the beads of fire dropping from my torch.
Go down, my little sister, follow the flowering flames.
Go down and make trade with the forbidden flower.
Go down to the ground and live among the dry leaves,
lying on a coarse mat and leaning against a colored pillow;
go down to the ground and live among the dry leaves.
Sending broken pieces of plate skimming thru the air
to fall on top of a hill,
to fall into the lap of the young girl,
the moon maiden come from the edge of the sky.
The husk of the seeds falls past the edge of the winnowing pan,
winnowed by an old woman on the edge of the outer veranda.

A lot of noise is made by the small children in the morning—
it is good to see their health,
their active bright yellow-brown bodies.

Give me none of that hot lime-powder mixture.
Give me instead the good-quality kind.
I don't want a bad-tempered girl,
a girl who always laughs is the one for me.
To borrow the claw of a small squirrel,
to borrow the hand of a small dwarf,
to borrow a small partridge from the top of the hill:
I am stepping over a big branch.
Today the two of us bale water with our hands—
we walk while sitting, going on hands and feet like crabs
cautiously toward a heap of gravel downstream.
In one gulp I swallow a whole winnowing pan full of food.

Go back, bees, go back;
return together with me, return.
Return, soul, together with me, return,
feet linked with feet, hands with hands linked.
Go back, bees, go back.
Bring news that the flower of the barley is greatly blossoming.
Come, bees, come,
do not forget our honey tree.
To pluck and take the *jaring* leaf,
to take the *krangan darud* leaf,
to snatch the souls, to take them back—I return,
feet linked with feet, hands with hands linked.

FIVE POEMS

ALLEN GROSSMAN

MY MARKMAN

I do not live by the sea but I have
   a friend who lives by the sea. On him
      the wind sheds images of the far shore

When he walks in the wind. On me the wind
   does not shed images, but I know of
      the far shore because he tells me of it.

Where he walks the Monarchs in their season
   come across tacking and swooping over
      the wave crests from the far shore, and then over

The salt marsh and the sea grass, one by one
   battering toward sleep in the Sierra Madre.
      Also whole days come to him on the wind

To which he gives a name, such as Storm Day
   or Wash Day or Death Day. He marks each one
      with a clear mark, a term. In winter he

Takes account of the six wings of the snow.
   On the far shore where gulls nest in the clearness
      of his thinking are treasuries of snow

And the wild horns from which spill butterflies.
  I love my markman who lives by the sea
    on whom the winds shed images he knows

I love him for waking and for the time,
  the whole days, and for the Monarch on the
    wind road to the mother mountain of sleep.

FOR PLATH

I
My serious distress exhausts the mean device
By which I have survived you, and betrays
Your elegist born with you in a bad year;
But with his death still in his hand.

Going the obscure way by the light
Of a rich branch, under the Elm Tree
Fruitful of treasons, I draw my sword
Against the air. Easy the descent.

Great souls admire your careful wounds—
Clamorous, imperial, extinct in multitudes;
Before and after, up stream and down,
Tu Marcellus eris, numberless.

II
And see the gardens that they here devise
Who have no occupation now but love,
Gardens of great grieving, gardens of night,
The young forever moving their fair hands.

Hail! You who have picked the dexter way,
The Sacred Grove, inheritors of Persephone:
Jephthah's daughter, flowers in her hair,
Pallas, himself a flower, Galahad

And Isaac, gigantic questioners,
Greet now another by the right of wounds
Come down among you. Let this fame too
Be writ in the iron book and locked.

III

Madness is easy. But the reascent,
The closing of the wound, the wrestling match,
Heaven and Hell, honor and names, tears
And unoffending sleep, this is the labor

The matter of rising from this clear air
To that mysterious sun. The gates stand open.
Before me the white Elm and the Dread Fountain.
Who would drink? Who would revisit?

For what was given has been taken back
As in the aberration of starlight
And we hear it depart, like a wind rising,
Or a thunderous closing of doors.

IV

In this time of mighty funerals a vision:
Four children in four corners of the field
Weeping white tears on the green grass
Without sorrow, and sleeping the starrry night.

A CLOUDY NIGHT

He resolved to say nothing he did not know.
It was a cloudy night.

                              A half-formed moon
Inside its dirty atmospheric sack

Uttered no intelligible sound. The oak leaves
Just rearranged themselves, like a lineage
Preparing to receive a new soul.

That night
He saw that the moon was his near neighbor—
A human moon.

So many things entered in
The following a simple track under
A human moon—the cold, the dark, the wet

Air—that at first he could say nothing. Then
The words that came were more a history
Than a song. . . . At last, the moon was shaken
Out of its sack.

He sat down by gleaming
Moonlight in the odd angle at which he
Found himself, and thought:

A singular thing
Came to mind—a perfect countenance with a moon-
Like mark on its brow.

Then he said to the moon,
"I want to take whatever you are to me
Inside me." And his mouth fell silent

Like an unbandaged wound found healed.

SALT TRADE ODE

The salt merchants beat drums to signal their arrival. They arranged their
salt in piles and went back out of sight. The gold traders then came out
of their mines and caves with their gold and put the amount they were
willing to offer beside each pile of salt. Then they went out of sight. The
salt merchants returned and considered the offers. The process of bar-
gaining continued until the salt and gold traders were both satisfied.

Sometimes the gold traders were in such need of salt that they were
willing to pay as much as two weights of gold for each weight of salt. At

times, when they could not get any pure salt they existed by using the ashes of plants, and by eating the meat and drinking the blood of such animals (and humans) as they could capture.

They knew from personal experience that they could live without gold but not without salt.—William W. Boddie, *The Silent Trade of Timbuktoo*

I
Blue fallen Jacaranda, the night rains, sleep
Almost to extinction—
And then desire (the mourning dove, infant
Suspiring in flutes) and tall sheep with brilliant
Garbage tied in their long hair the shepherds
Summon with a curse. The pounding mattock
Of the sullen gardener begins to wake you,
Under your afghan, your hound still folded
At your feet like sleep. The salt light enters
My eye and lodges—one grain at a time.

II
All day, and much of the night, my thoughts come in,
Burdened, silent, cruel—salt laden
Camels to Timbuktoo. Foul, relentless
Caravans from the North,
Resting infrequently, and without plan,
At unknown stations, transgressing untaxed
The boundaries of the great kings of the way
Bring in the salt.
The wind blows but the salt camels come in,
Thousands upon thousands till death end the need.

III
There are great thinkers, as there are bright stars.
They are not more to me than rain blurring
The window, and less, by dim magnitudes,
Than your averted eyes.
But the camels and the camel men bring salt,
Killing sleep with the harsh manners of the North
And the vile songs of Tripoli.
Salt is like thinking—strong savor of rock—
That cannot be put off,
When the rain stops, and the great stars blaze down.

IV

Eye blinded by seeing, market of tears,
To Timbuktoo comes down what is, that pit,
That hollow, where all things come down, and stunned
In rapture turn to salt. Cowries and gold
We give, embroidery of all flowers,
A sad nation of traders
Feeding its sad salt hunger with the tales
Of the camel men. They sing what they know
Leaving me
Poorer, and in a world less reconciled.

V

The winds blow. Rains shift to the South—
And not return.
A sort of patience, and a sort of light;
Half light, and wrathful patience without peace.
The lions in their dream come down to salt
From the high Mountains of Air. Where are you?
How could I lose you in so small a house?
Either you are in the kitchen,
Or in the garden, or lying down under
Your afghan, or gone away with your hound.

VI

They go, deadly visions, the salt trade done,
Up the wind's black track, leaving the salt light.
In the seared eye of Timbuktoo, wind's weir,
I stir and startle at thought's ebb and cease:
To identify the objects in the landscape,
That gives pleasure—
The manifest, and the unmanifest, tree;
The dim salt cliff, so womanlike; the barren
Hill and shade;
The caves of absence by the estranging tide.

VII

Hysteria at the crossroads. Real tears.
The end of no thought, but thought's end—last salt.
Where are you? Gone with the rain's romantic
Hue and cry. At the moment of tears, found gone.

Hysteria at the crossing
Where two ways thunder in contestation.
Shall I leave the city Timbuktoo, where
Lions roam the lion city? Sister,
Return
And let me see you, as the light declines.

LAMENT

Go down

(Forsaking the lagoons of bridged Atlantis)

To the Mid-Atlantic ridge
                                where are the crazed
Magnetic fields, and roped sheets, and stains
(The disordered fabric of the volcanic
Bed chamber) and the gigantic vermicular
Testimonies
                and stars upon the great
Principle of the solid world—the original
Torment trace.

                        Go down, for down is the way.
And grapple one stone syllable
Of all that frozen love's discourse
Onto an iron dredge
                        and on it rise
(Borne on the enormous weight of its desire
For light and the air)
                        until it explodes
Upon the deck amid the astonished crew.

Then empty out the nets disposed about
Your person, and fill them with the pieces
Of that one vast syllable
                        and carry them

To Cahokia in East Saint Louis, where
My father was born who is dying now

(Go you. I have no words. I am his son.)

Place them on the top of Monk's Mound

(He was an honest man and mute as stone.)

                         and let

Them off like a siren.

AN UNKNOWN DISTANCE

STEPHEN EMERSON

Are your remarks, so called, "savage"? How is the action on your machine? What experience do you have when you listen to Bud Powell? How is the action on your machine. Are there some circumstances that are so out of the ordinary that your conduct in them is beyond criticism? (Name one that is not a war.) Show something to your friend, i.e., find him. Change the record.

Rudd found Herbie Nichols and went to him twice weekly for instruction, thence learning to improvise over chords that would otherwise have eluded him, or anyone. Where is Herbie Nichols, would you know him if you heard him, or is that it. If you test your experience rigorously enough, do you have any experience other than that of testing. Discuss the advantages and disadvantages of serial prose.

Why this interest in questions? Is it a rhetoric or structure that catches, or are you inclined to be inquisitive, or not inquisitive. (Possibly years of asking no questions, to have certainty of no lies, well up for release at such time as no lies possible.) Terriffic. Go buy yourself some overalls, then wear them for a while. After that, work hard in the field ten years. Then come back and ask any question that remains interesting.

She stops at a place you think you know, to get something. Yet where you end up is a quite different place. You have never been here before, but everyone else has. In two rooms people are making love. It is a kind of restaurant. Her name is Herbie Nichols.

We were sitting around
chewing the fat.

The wine
tasted like shit.

Mary is
a big drag.

Do you like blow jobs? No that's not
my bag.

Spike. Some fucking shit about Spike. Spike out by the pond, with
the horses, doin some fishin. Get a little hooch, a bright night, go
out and do some fishin. Wait for the catfish. Prop the pole on
sumpum, and wait for the line to drop. Talk about the old days.
We went down to the beach and drank seven cases of beer over one
week end. Dancing with you, his wife takes off her shirt. You should
have heard the way this guy could play guitar. I mean it. Just like
Steve Cropper. Dickie Betts. Scottie bla bla. Now just sits around
somewhere drinks beer. Pumps gas. Out at Wendell's, one time, guy
comes up, in the rain, honks his fuckin horn, and waits. You know
old Wendell. Just ignores it. Guy leans on that shiteatin horn of his.
Wendell goes out, guy wants fuckin directions. Wendell sends him
eighteen miles the wrong way. Spike is still talking. Down near
Columbus . . . no tonight she leaves the shirt on. Wants to leave.
The fire burns low. The hooch runs out. Spike keeps talking. Next
full moon, we'll do some catfishin.

I keep remembering that room in the hospital. Lying awake in it at
night, in the heat, three beds on the left, one to the right, the
windows at each end, space in front, the large doorway. I never lay
awake in it at night, was always asleep before they put the lights
out. The guy to the left still wanting to talk, and smoking, his arm
hanging in traction. In the middle of the night in that room, each
night, at four, I woke up, calling for a painkiller. Let's say that each
night when I woke up in it then, a single chord was sounded on a
vibraharp. Which would be less vague, more dramatic, and is,
therefore, what happened. I was stuck in that bed, people coming
to me, nurses, clean, starched, and feminine, constantly leaning over
me, all their dealings with me required them to lean over, friends
fading out, from that bed, tethered to my leg, I watched the world

take place around me. I remember lying awake all night in that room I was never in, some exotic place, drugged, awake all night, and somewhere maybe in Africa. Watching the world.

Once your man has gotten by you, there isn't darn much you can do. You can try and catch up with him. Or you can try to reach in after the ball without hitting him, or you can try and get the ball on the way up. Either of those he's gonna call you. When he's gotten around you, there isn't darn much you can do.

Lennie Tristano: OK, cut it with these references to musicians no one has thought of for twenty years. How about this: I can hear hitchhikers: "Really enjoyable inasmuch as . . ." "Yah. I hear you." Screaming as car passes them.

There are only two limits on her happiness: him, and his girl-friend. But that doesn't count herself. That's right.

Phenomenal. The way the piano chord glazed the saxophone part. I kind of like, tapping the ash against the edge of the bottle cap, onto her leg, I thought I liked using a little ashtray. One ninety, he said, for the two drinks that cost ninety cents each. I handed him a dollar eighty and got twenty cents change. When I saw Jim's dog, I wondered what would explain what it was doing outside. Walking to the door, I saw a note: Folks: Please don't let dog out.—Jim

He said that to *me*. Dig it: Me. Right? He turned back to the game. Three tens. Oh Susan *I'm sorry*. He realized he'd knocked her with his elbow. He gestured with his hand. You know me, Susan. But she wasn't Susan, Susan was his wife. He kept calling her by his wife's name. Jesus fuck *me*: why *am* I calling you Susan. Really, hopeless, absolutely. I can imagine if *Susan*.

Taking the mailer the shirt had come in, he put the book into it that he'd been waiting to send until he had a mailer, and looked for string to tie it with, since it was large for the book. His mind's eye showed him the string in a drawer, where it shouldn't have been, so he looked not there but in other cupboards, drawers, and shelves, more likely settings. He kept looking, and when he could think of no new spots, he looked again where he'd already looked. After about an hour he did go to the drawer that had initially occurred to him and, removing the string, tied the package up.

The joke
fell flat.

He was fast, but he sounded
like shit.

Didn't you know that you could see each person by looking at
    his face?

If you can find an old saw that cuts,
use it.

"At his best he . . ." "Do you want to book?"—laid on top of the scene like some kind of space blanket: plop. Sure, we want to book. In his desire to demonstrate the comfort he felt, the impermeability of his surging mood by her previously disastrous presence, whom he wanted to fuck, he issued a series of quips that grew cornier and cornier, his position now that of the would-be and oblivious charmer, telling dumb jokes while the gorgeous one yawns, whereupon she left, plop. The reason was, she wanted to book, because he was not at his best she did not know him to have. Plop. Plop.

One day the reserve by which he was known would give way and all that it concealed would be exposed. But then he would be a different person.

I was up here and the fear was down there, didn't know what was holding me up. The words kept turning into shapeless lumps, my mind wandering to my childhood, a hilarity that came off summer camp had no purchase on the present moment. I wanted to respect her body like it was the last thing on earth, but it wasn't there. I stayed up, the words drying now and crumbling, each minute I spent I knew something more about what held me, I thought the fear might in time be neutralized.

It's later that you're sorry.
Right now you're not sorry.

She called it a tire iron, when what she really meant was, a lug wrench. The term seemed right, but it wasn't. He said, I love you, when it meant . . . and he meant. . . .

Didn't understand how anyone's view of relationships could be so saccharine. Now, at the edge, a perfume remembered from eleven years back. Marriage, what it could do to you. She was married, she didn't understand, it was so saccharine, everyone would have to come to terms with it, how the perfume still could smell, had no clear being any more than marriage.

Mary, there is something I must tell you. Mary, it is not true that nothing is plenty for me, Mary. It's not. I want, Mary, you. Mary I want you. I want to make a life together, Mary, the two of us, you, and me.

Let me put this another way. They used to say, I got plenty of nothing, and that's good enough. I must differ. Mary, that's wrong, Mary: dead wrong. The reason I can say that, Mary, is: I want you. If all I've got is nothing, I don't have you. And I want you. And am dissatisfied.

Feel the guilt as grit against top of throat, the day bad, a saxophonist running irrelevant obligattos on it, threatening to become the actual substance. Then there was the whole question of ethics, independent of how something felt, which would have to be dismissed. Her mouth tasted bad, around a carton of cigarettes, maybe some beer gone flat in there waiting for her to swallow, not to mention that when you look at her you see your life.

I don't get it. Some great misery, in one's life is what we're after? Always going for that one. Smoking dope and _____; fucking and _____; your heart broken and _____; huh? Listening to Albert Ayler (Ornette Coleman); watching friend's face crack into twisted pieces (Lennie Tristano's). It's okay if they're not in love with you (no it isn't). I want to make a life together, Mary, the two of us, you, and me. Is that okay? There is a slight relief when it is expressed, feel slightly better when I rub my problem on the head. Several times that day his mood dropped (fell) as his _____ performed as _____. Fuck you, X, Y, Z, and a few others. Where were you when I was worried about _____?

And so there is you and the "other." That is an elaborate term for someone else, or an object with which you come into contact, so called. The saxophone, for example, which is a toy, made of plastic, or "her," to use a personification honored, as we say, by time. Also known as, she, or, you. The rhythm you wish to play at is spicy, a sensory term associated with, Latin, a geographical area, or, "culture," of which you know nothing, the rhythm also identified with a playful, ultimately predictable toying with expectation.

At the dance where the girls and boys had never met, each sex grouped at the appropriate bathroom. On the bus on the way in, at least one boy mentioned bathroom, and the reason became clear immediately: if a situation with, or without, a girl, became at all perplexing, you went to the bathroom, where the other boys were, and approval and rebellion were available simultaneously. That such an avoidance obscured the actual purpose of the dance went unnoticed. Your real curiosity was with what was going on at the bathroom, and not what might develop with a girl, that ground being so unknown as to be dubious and negligible. The chance of getting laid was nonexistent, and given that, the minimal hope of necking was unattractive, as it seemed to refer to some Hollywood notion of romance that obviously didn't apply.

After going several times to the bathroom, once to escape what we called a "dog," another time a tedious awkwardness that had set in with a second partner, and finding the bathroom itself uneventful, uncertainty as rife there as in the ballroom, I found myself dancing with a really pleasant girl. She was tall, maybe taller than I was, not overly attractive, though her full hips and shoulders moved with grace and the definition of her face instantly appealed. We talked about what proved common to us, a town I'd often visited that was near where she lived, and her brother, who went to school with me. The conversation lacked any urgency, and I sensed that she didn't take me seriously, whatever that meant, that I was a social inferior, but the sense came from an indifference she projected, that I did too, as the only thing I knew how. So finally there was a kind of comfort between us, though I didn't know what to make of her, couldn't decide if she liked me, was she attractive or would the others think so, still our time together had an ease within which she showed no dissatisfaction, no promptings toward other boys or the bathroom. And as it became time to leave, she said she would walk with me to the bus. Saying goodbye to her, I felt an affection, maybe gratitude, that I couldn't voice, so after saying that we might cross paths sometime in her town, which she clearly knew we wouldn't, I turned, and she turned, and, puzzled, I walked the remaining distance to the bus.

SIX POEMS

MIROSLAV HOLUB

Translated from the Czech by Stuart Friebert

BRIEF REFLECTION ON IDENTITY

Day after day nothing repeats itself.
   Not rivers, not prophets, not goats.

And if the same today is the same tomorrow,
   it won't be that way, all things don't
   stay the same all the time. Because
   as soon as one thing changes, all other
   things change. Things are not alone,
   they closely depend on other things,

Or partly depend on them. . . . so that, you
   know, I mean we don't get. . .

Even the prophets are a part of this fixed
   relationship. So are words. So are goats,
   so is milk. So is blood.

So it's considerably difficult
   to recognize your own words, your own
   blood, your own prophet and your goat.

Considerably difficult. But again and again
   we try to, so that we don't get goats
   from prophets and blood from milk.

And now let's affirm the identity of things,
   we come in twos, when we're gone there'll be
   a double to take our place and we'll all
   march slowly into the darkness.

BRIEF REFLECTION ON THE MUTINY OF VIADUCTS

I've always felt that on the other side
   of a tunnel there should be something different
   from what's on this side.

Similarly
   a viaduct should run from somewhere
   to somewhere else, and looking through the archway
   it'd be fine to see something sort of
   unexpected, some newness, sky blueness.

Sadly it seems there's just mud behind the viaduct
   as well as in front of it; that it's forbidden
   to lean out of train windows, even when you're through
   the tunnel; if the plague's behind the archway
   it'll be in front in a little while.

But maybe there's no such thing as elsewhere.

And tunnels, arches, and viaducts cunningly hide
   this embarrassment.

It's imperative that tunnels, arches, and viaducts
   understand this. It's imperative they draw
   consequences from this. It's imperative
   they revolt. That they go—thundering
   with their boulders, ripping with their
   concrete, wailing with their steel rods,
   get up and go—

Somewhere else?
No. Just keep moving
along.

BRIEF REFLECTION ON COLORS

Blue is certainly number four or even
    the vowel o, including birds and smoke
    of native Ithaca.

White is number one then, same as the vowel
    i, long as it's white and cold and not aligned.
    Which also means the future of flowers,
    the past books; blindness of the earth,
    unseen till now. Silence.

Black can be number nine, long as it's not in the order
    of very refined numbers, even numbers fade
    if they're sophisticated; you too may be black
    sometimes, blackness can also occur in
    skull-like cliffs and caves; yes, and in the order
    and anger of matter.

Red on the other hand is three and five, however
    it's lighter, more brown. The letter a is red
    like the open mouth of a small animal. Also,
    battle is red and Faust's pen and love
    in summer. And the fanfare of hope.

Therefore, we have an equation in four colors.
    $4=1.9-5$, likewise olive groves by the sea
    during the equinox and the period between
    two wars, which happens once a year at most.

No wonder the authorities don't love poetry and guards
    linger in the shadows where nobody can see
    how worried they are about the strict order of

Colors.

BRIEF REFLECTION ON TARGETS

We have targets so there's something to hit.
We have targets to have something to hit.

And there are stone faces at the sides to see
    if we hit the targets the way we're supposed to.
    Stony faces mostly of plaster but even
    though they are they can see if we hit
    the way we're supposed to.

If we don't hit the way we're supposed to
    the stony faces will hit us. Because
    one has to shoot. And we are something good
    to hit, children. There's no danger
    of the bullet bouncing back.

So that there's actually no lack of targets. Never.

And let nobody think they can aim
    at the side, I mean at a stony face.

Because, let's see, there's never a lack of them.
    There's never been a lack of them in the past,
    and never will be in the future.
Let's see, there must always be stony faces.

Because without them there'd be nobody
    to judge if we hit the way we're supposed to
    and what the target really is.

BRIEF REFLECTION ON DEATH

Many people are busy
as if they weren't born yet. Meanwhile
William Burroughs, asked by a student
if he believes in postmortal life
said:
        —And how do you know that you haven't died already?

BRIEF REFLECTION ON LOGIC

The big problem is everything has
    its own logic. Everything you can
    think of, whatever falls on your head.
    Somebody will always add the logic.
    In your head or on it.

Even a cylinder makes sense, at least
    in that it's not a cube. Even a cleft
    makes sense, maybe just because
    it's not a big mountain.

A special logic must be assigned to cylinders
    that pretend to be cubes. And clefts
    that think they're big mountains.

The logic of these things is in fact that
    they strip other things of their meaning.

This reflection isn't abstract.

It's in view
    of recent history.

TREES, THEIR LEGACY OF GREEN

PAAVO HAAVIKKO

Translated from the Finnish by R. Sieburth

TRANSLATOR'S NOTE. *Paavo Haavikko, born in Helsinki in 1931, has worked in the real estate business and as a financial consultant. Currently an editor for the Otava publishing firm, he is considered one of Finland's most significant contemporary poets. In addition to some eight volumes of verse, Haavikko has written a number of novels, short stories, and plays. The collection from which the poems here are taken,* Trees, Their Legacy of Green *("Puut, kaikki heidän poydällä"), was published in 1966. In making these versions I have been greatly assisted by the German translations of M. P. Hein, brought out by Suhrkamp in 1973.*

You can be sure
    it was her
& nobody else
    you met, in person:
the World,
           not as one says some vague
                    allegorical entity
    involved in ancient rites,
which is why you caught almost nothing when
  she mentioned her name:
    she talks fast, slurring
everything at once.

        •

Trees, nights getting longer
bit
    by bit, barely noticeable.
And the dark
    does not stop the trees
        from rustling.
Still, it is sad. Like someone
    talking to a child, trying
        to hide something
it already knows.

           •

There are many wise men yet on the other hand
        not a single case of madness among trees.
    After writing the hardest thing
is reading.

           •

Faulkner, Early in the Morning

The old man is tired of talking
    incessantly about himself.
Who has answered all the letters
        saying nothing.
No Chekov.
Who forgot his name.
When a man dies, he once again goes
    to his car, to his wife, to work.
The motor won't start, the wife won't
    wake up, it's must too early.
He is dead.

           •

Many books remain unread when
    it is not clear
        where so and so sleeps, where he gets his money,
        with whom he sleeps,

how he gets away with life, the only
    adventure
        I indulge in,

Life & Works & Love, abstractions—
    read no further
        where they end

           •

We
    must go on living, even where
      nations have been
laid to rest, or rather, next to these
    in fields reserved for suicides & braggarts
        with dogs for neighbors
in plots so nourished by presumption
    that the trees,
      rowan, birch, linden & fir
      flourish,
one must live here as life has here been lived
    for four thousand years,
      four hundred of which in this region,
        with lower lip hanging,
meditatively.

          •

September, and when the grass makes a racket
    and the shadows crash
      down from trees.
    The world, a war memorial
      erected
and seeded, green.
    Which more and more people want to see.
So that it becomes unbearable to hear them tell
    how they were there
      and saw it all.

        •

My grandfather, the Kaiser, was, as you know,
    crazy,
      wrote poems in the company
      of others.
You want war,
    you can have it.
          You march stiffly
into battle,

hysteric, chronic
victors.
        Why talk. I quote the poem:

The fog is so thick the water
        disappears from the bridge.
Flowers break into a frenzy
                when they die
                        for no reason.

              •

Lacking all else, take a pair of
      stones to bed,
washed white by the sea,
        they breathe, sea-smell within them,
take a pair of white stones
when your bed gets too broad alone.

You want your own life. Good. To be
      your own man.
Careful. Worms wait precisely for this.
      To live as long
          as you are young.
Wrong. A thousand blind eyes bite the image apart.

A child's fear within you, fear
      breathing the dark
        when the games break up.

              •

I see what is outside, the stove fire
      burns in the window
        behind the rain, the smoke, the green alder,
I reflect, my life, already back of
      so many wars:
The door opening behind us, the frame in which
      you see me
        how I come
              & go, before I
                turn away & proceed,
the house, the love & the

happy days
  hereafter
      come apart.

                    •

I like slow things, the way they happen
  again & again.
Like, say, water as it warms & reaches
  boil.
        Which takes time.

The balance is not in the stillness
  but the way
      the water pours from you
          as you move from the sea.

THREE POEMS

JORGE CARRERA ANDRADE

Translated from the Spanish by Donald D. Walsh

LIVING TONGUES

The tree lets fall
its green syllables
that translate
the language of the woods,

written wisdom
in the veins of the leaves.
Fate can be read
in the green-making lines.

The rough-kneed tree bark,
tenderness in rows,
shelters a reserve
of tenderness.

The briefest tongue,
as it flies through the air,
utters its word,
prophecy of woods.

THE ALCHEMY OF LIFE

An old man lives inside me, contriving my death.
At his breath the years turn to ashes,
the fruits break down their sugars,
and the hoarfrost visits my organic labyrinth.

Wind, needles and pale substances
are manipulated by this guest in ambush.
At times, while I sleep, I hear a gentle liquid
going drop by drop into his pitcher.

He has bathed my skin with his yellow chemistry.
He has changed the climate of my hand.
In the place of my face, his wrinkled face
I find in the mirrors.

He conspires in the depths
where the bowels tremble—a weary animal—
and amid green matter and icy retorts,
contriving my death, he lets the years go by.

I NAME THE STONE

Do my senses perceive
only the outer world?
Is there no sign of the dark cave where lives
                the silent man
                burdened with dreams,
wounded by the rose and by the sword
and lost in a labyrinth of mirrors?

When I go down to the bottom of myself,
objects lay siege to me.
The clock gnaws on time's infinite bread.
I name the stone: translate it anguish.
I name the birds: it means the voyage
of uneasiness adrift.

I name the corn: the return toward the beginning.
Each thing I name is only a code
for the dark language
of the depths of myself.

KANSAS / OR DECEMBER POEM

ELIZABETH MARRAFFINO

somewhere in kansas you told me deep things

you surprised me   it was december
your touch surprised me   like the first hour of spring
      or april's first distant bird

            crying

                crying

what was the war like   i asked
you couldn't answer me   a man with such strong arms
i wonder how you survived it   a man like a flower
breaking open
      to the slightest touch of sun

that night your life haloed you with black light
                              sad light

until you smiled as i said   there are still such beautiful things
                  look at the kansas plain
      half sea   half sky at twilight no beginning or end

i for one, didn't think love could come again
but your kisses fell like falling stars
even the midnight cattle were shining
  to the right and the left of us

in front of me deep snow gathered on the road

most of all it surprises me after you
 this loneliness
  settling on my shoulders
   like windy kansas dust

NOTES ON CONTRIBUTORS

Last year, WALTER ABISH was writer-in-residence at Wheaton College in Norton, Massachusetts, and Visiting Butler Professor of English at the University of Buffalo. The recipient of an Ingram Merrill Foundation grant for 1978, his most recent book is *In the Future Perfect* (1977), a collection of short fiction published by New Directions.

JORGE CARRERA ANDRADE was born in Quito, Ecuador, in 1903. The late Thomas Merton wrote of him: "Humanity, tenderness and wit in the sense of *'esprit'* characterize the innocence and seriousness of Jorge Carrera Andrade. He is one of the most appealing of the fine Latin American poets of our century. One is tempted to call him an incarnation of the genius of his humble and delightful country, Ecuador." DONALD D. WALSH's most recent book of translations with New Directions, in collaboration with Robert Pring-Mill, is *Apocalypse and Other Poems* by Ernesto Cardenal (1977).

A leading younger Mexican poet, HOMERO ARIDJIS is also his country's ambassador to the Netherlands. "Exaltation of Light" is from his 1976 collection, *Quemar las Naves* (*"Burn the Boats"*). The translation is by ELIOT WEINBERGER, editor of the literary magazine *Montemora*. An earlier selection of Aridjis's work appeared in *ND29*.

The British novelist J. G. BALLARD is well known in this country for his many books of speculative fiction. "The Intensive Care Unit" is his first appearance in these pages.

A London pediatrician, MARTIN BAX also edits the literary magazine *Ambit*. New Directions brought out his novel, *The Hospital Ship*, in 1976.

For information about MARCEL BLECHER, see the translator's note preceding his "Adventures in Immediate Unreality."

180

Among the many volumes by JEAN COCTEAU obtainable in English translation are *The Holy Terrors* and *The Infernal Machine and Other Plays* from New Directions. His poem sequence *Leoun* appeared in *ND17*. PERRY OLDHAM, who translated the prose poems included here, is the author of a book of war poems, *Vinh Long*, published by Northwoods Press.

Long resident in Kyoto, CID CORMAN is the editor and publisher of *Origen*, now into its 4th series. His most recent books are a volume of essays, *At Their Word*, and a selected lyrics, *Root Song*, both published by Black Sparrow, and a collection of poetry, *Antics*, from Origen Press. In addition, he is editing for Mushinsha Books, in Eric Sackheim's translation series, the collected poems of ANDRÉ DU BOUCHET. For further information, see Corman's note preceding du Bouchet's "Six Poems."

Twenty-seven years old, STEPHEN EMERSON has spent the last year or so in northern California, Alaska, North Carolina, and Key West, working as a road-striper, editor, and librarian, and traveling in between. He has published in several small magazines and is now completing his first book, of which "An Unknown Distance" is the opening section.

A selection of GAVIN EWART's poems appeared in *ND33*. Born in London in 1916, he is the author of four books of verse: *The Gavin Ewart Show* and *Be My Guest* from Trigram Press, and *No Fool Like an Old Fool* and *Or Where a Young Penguin Lies Screaming* from Gollancz. He is the editor as well of *New Poems 1977–78: A P.E.N. Anthology of Contemporary Poetry*, published by Hutchinson of London.

A longtime contributor, ALLEN GINSBERG's sequence of poems "Don't Grow Old" appeared in *ND36*. See his introduction for a brief discussion of the nine young poets whose work he selected for "Ginsberg's Choice."

ALLEN GROSSMAN teaches English and American literature at Brandeis University. He is the author of *And the Dew Lay All Night on My Branch* (Aleph Press), as well as two other books of verse currently out of print. The poems included here are part of his newest collection, now in formation.

Information on PAAVO HAAVIKKO can be found in the translator's note preceding his "Trees, Their Legacy of Green." RICHARD SIEBURTH teaches comparative literature at Harvard. He is the author of a book on Ezra Pound and Remy de Gourmont, due out from Harvard University Press this fall.

An earlier story by W. J. HOLINGER, "Infants," appeared in *ND35*. He has also contributed work to such periodicals as *North American Review* and *The Western Humanities Review*.

MIROSLAV HOLUB is an immunologist currently on the staff of the Institut Klincké A Experimentální Medicíny in Prague, as well as the author of several volumes of poetry, puppet plays, and children's stories. His latest book in English, *Notes from a Clay Pigeon*, was translated by Ian Milner and published by Secker and Warburg (London). STUART FRIEBERT directs the writing program at Oberlin College and is coeditor of *Field* magazine. He was assisted in his translations by Daniel Simko, a native of Gzechoslovakia now a student at Oberlin.

EDUARDO GUDIÑO KIEFFER's novel *Guía de Pecadores* ("A Sinner's Guidebook") was published by Editorial Losada (Buenos Aires) in 1972. Though an extremely prolific and best-selling writer in his native Argentina, only a few short pieces by him have been translated into English, published in *TriQuarterly* and the Center for International Relations' *Review*. RONALD CHRIST and GREGORY KOLOVAKOS are a translating team whose most recent venture is Mario Vargas Llosa's *Captain Pantoja and the Special Service*.

Poetry by ELIZABETH MARRAFFINO has appeared in such diverse magazines as *Choice, The Nation, Hand Book, New York Quarterly, Sojourner, Sun,* and *Toothpaste*. She has organized and directed poetry reading in the Berkshires, read widely in the New York area, and is now forming a poetry/rock-and-roll band called Kali-Flower.

PAUL PINES's first volume of poetry, *Onion*, was brought out by Mulch Press in 1971. He was a CAPS Fellow for 1976 and has published in numerous little magazines. Currently, he is putting together a prose book based on his working experiences in saloons and focusing on the cultural vortex that was the Tin Palace, a jazz club on the Bowery he owned and operated in the early '70s.

For information on NÉLIDA PIÑON, see the translator's note preceding her story, "Natural Frontier." GIOVANNI PONTIERO teaches in the Department of Spanish and Portuguese studies at the University of Manchester. He is the author of a critical study on Piñon that appeared in *Review 76*.

EDOUARD RODITI's most recent book is *The Delights of Turkey* (New Directions, 1977), a collection of twenty tales every bit as engaging and erudite as "Woman to Her Midget Lover. . . ."

"The Honey Tree Song of Raseh" was originally published in CAROL RUBENSTEIN's *Poems of Indigenous Peoples of Sarawak: Some of the Songs and Chants*, a special monograph of the Sarawak Museum in Kuching, Malaysia, issued in two parts in 1973, in a project sponsored by the Ford Foundation. Ms. Rubenstein's own poetry has appeared in such magazines as *Vincent, Black Sun, W.I.N.*, and *New Wilderness Letter*. JEROME ROTHENBERG's *A Seneca Journal* was published earlier this year by New Directions.

VITTORIO SERENI's long poem "A Vacation Place" appeared in *ND27*. Born in Luino in 1913, he now lives in Milan, where he edits the prestigious *Lo Specchio* poetry series for the Italian publishing house of Mondadori. FRANK JUDGE has translated the work of a number of contemporary Italian poets, among them Bonazzi, Cimatti, and di Biasio. He lives in Rochester, New York.

A poet associated with the early Beat movement, CARL SOLOMON's books include *Mishaps, Perhaps* (1966) and *More Mishaps* (1968), both published by City Lights.

RYUICHI TAMURA, born in 1923, founded the magazine *The Waste Land* in 1947 and with its contributors helped give direction to postwar Japanese poetry. His first collection of poems, *Four Thousand Days and Nights*, appeared in 1956; its title, he has explained, refers to the ten-year period from the end of the war to the publication of the book. A selection of his work was included in *ND22*. HIROAKI SATO's newest book of translations, *Howling at the Moon:*

Poems of Sakutaro Hagiwara, is scheduled for publication by the University of Tokyo Press.

H. C. TEN BERGE, one of the foremost younger poets of the Netherlands, edits the avant-garde literary magazine *Raster*. "The Other Sleep," his first work to appear in the United States, is from his book *De Witte Sjamaan ("The White Shaman")*, published by De Bezige Bij, Amsterdam, in 1973. PETER NIJMEIJER is himself a poet and a leading translator of contemporary Netherlandic literature.

STEPHEN VINCENT is poetry editor of *The San Francisco Review of Books,* in which his interview with MICHAEL MCCLURE originally appeared in a somewhat expanded form. McClure's latest book of poetry is *Antechamber and Other Poems* (New Directions, 1978).